NIGHT WING

By

Christine Westwood

CHAPTER 1

The moors lay like dark velvet under a starlit sky. The long and glittering line of the ocean shimmered on the distant horizon. I smiled, recalling the stupidity of the customs men. In their haste to stow the contraband from the Marlena and get to a night's drinking at the inn, they hadn't seen me and my raiding party until we were standing over them with muskets, bidding them fill the wagon they had just unloaded. The century may have turned and King George may be on the throne but Cornwall still had its share of smugglers and robbers. It was sheer laziness that the pickings weren't secured in Customs House but thrown in a temporary lockup for pirates like us to sniff out and pounce on.

I could see the silhouettes of a handful of my new recruited sailors as they bound the officers and locked them in the rundown shed where the booty had barely touched ground. I heard their voices carrying over the whisper of the night sea. A few paces and down the slope from me stood the rest of the men. They formed a circle around my trusted quartermaster Flynn and the two thieving privateers who thought they could cheat me. Generally, men were too afraid to cross me, pirate Queen Meg. When it happened, I had to put paid to it, and quickly. I set off down the slope. The men parted hurriedly as I approached, their whispers stilled.

I pointed at Ripley, one of the privateers. "Did you take them?"

He grimaced, red rimmed eyes stark with terror. Flynn pushed him to his knees.

"Did you mark them?" I demanded.

"Mistress," he whimpered, "By accident only - careless - "

Flynn jerked his head in the direction of a pile of cloth. I took a couple of paces and bent over to finger the fine and costly silk gowns. Flynn had found them bundled behind the shed, not piled with the rest of the contraband. There was a streak of blood at the white collared neck of one, a smear on the sleeve of another. Ripley had been the only man to soil his hands in the skirmish with the officers. He had sliced a guard's throat, making a meal of it when a simple blow to the head would have done the job. He could hardly deny it was his bloody fingerprints that had grabbed the silks when he'd seen his chance.

I turned to Ripley, raising my voice so it carried over the night breeze and the sough of the waves.

"I bring you on board, give you a chance to join my crew and at first test, you fail."

Ripley crouched lower, dumb with fear. I turned to glare at his companion, Gerande.

"You didn't try to stop him?"

"I don't think he meant to rob you, ma'am, only keep the goods safe."

"Safe for himself."

The air prickled. From the corner of my eye I saw Gerande nudge Ripley with his foot, an inconsequential motion except for the glint of steel as Ripley pulled a knife from Gerande's boot.

Ripley leapt at me like a cornered dog, grabbing my arm to pull me to the ground. My dagger was in his chest before he drew another breath, his face a picture of surprise as his mouth coughed the blood out of him.

"The booty was mine," I said. "You spoiled it and you stole it."

I heard the scuffling feet of his companion, the whimper as he ran. My men, four seamen, two boys, another privateer, in short the whole raiding party, stopped Gerande in his tracks. Torches whipped smoke in the night air. I jerked my dagger, still warm and bloody, from Ripley's heart, picked up the bundle of silk and approached the group of sailors.

"She killed him!" Gerande's thick Breton accent choked with rage and fear. "He didn't steal nothing, we was going to put it in the pot with all the rest. Fair shares, right?"

I unsheathed my rapier. The blade tore across Gerande's shins and he went down like a broken mast.

I threw the bloodstained robes on the ground, silk rippling."What fair shares when thieves help themselves?"

I swung the blade around the group of men, inches from nose tips. The men flinched, boys jumped back.

"Pick those up and you'll meet the same fate."

The silence was a black hole in the night, broken by Gerande as he pissed himself where he lay on the dark ground. I threw my head back and laughed at the ring of white and stricken faces.

"Come, boys!" I rallied them. "Can't you tell a joke from Queen Meg? Of course the silks are yours, and the doubloons and fine claret and all the booty we gained. You're my buccaneers, aren't you? None of you are light fingered bastards are you? Thieves that steal from me and each other, breaking the pirate's code?"

I gave them a minute, until one then another risked a smile, a nod, a guffaw of relief. My voice rose.

"You're Queen Meg's boys, the richest, bravest boys on the seven oceans. Good work tonight, and welcome to your share of the plunder."

I sheathed the rapier as they began to murmur and nod back to me.

"Back on board to share the spoils." I flourished a wave and dropped a deep and mocking curtsey. "We'll crack a casket to celebrate."

I walked away from them, up the pale, snaking line of the hill track, and let out a long, shuddering breath. Ripley's face, the bubbling gasp of his last breath, grabbed at me. I turned to look down at the men as they hoisted the body. It was always the way, breaking in new crew, working all over again to keep up my reputation. Though I was Queen Meg, weather witch of the seven seas and quicker than any man with the rapier, in the world of piracy there are always rivals. I knew there were many who dreamed of dispatching me, as ruthlessly as I had that thieving privateer.

CHAPTER 2

I tapped the toe of my buckled shoe on the deck timbers, feeling the Night Wing gently rise and dip. This was the moment I loved, feeling the strong pull of my ship, readying to give herself to the sea. She sensed the wide ocean, as I did, beyond the narrow embrace of Looe harbour. Patiently, she held back as we left the shallows for the deep plunge of open water. Her prow pointed square to a long horizon with a grey line of dawn breaking along its edge.

My heart leapt to hear the windlass creak and the sail's whip, flung wide with the breeze. I was too restless to go below so I stepped my way past the deck hands to the fo'c'sle, taking my place behind Flynn as he spun the wheel to guide us out. Broad backed and a head taller than me, Flynn was quiet, fearless, a true sailor, with a fearsome roving eye for women in any port.

I hitched one foot up on a capstan, steadying myself to gaze at the soft line of clouds, rimmed with the pearl of early light. I touched the rough wool of Flynn's sleeve. He glanced at me.

"Still fair for the direction set, mistress?"

I nodded. "There'll be fine weather all the way. Though bitter cold when we reach the Norwegian Sea. I'll tell Cal to hand out extra rum and blankets."

I couldn't wait to be on open sea after the business with the thieves. The unnecessary killing made me uneasy, I hated the mess of it. Out on the ocean all was simple. I held control, Quartermaster Flynn and Bosun Cal beside me, the men in their place, the whip and crack of Night Wing's sails as we sped before the wind. At sea, the crew couldn't fail to bow, and, such is the nature of men, the bowing made them feel safe and happy. They knew the order of things, bound by ship and sail. They knew they were fed better than any other crew, healthier and richer in spoils.

There were no floggings and games of torture on the Night Wing, the men were respected for good work and loyalty. It was very simple, they were killed and gone the moment that loyalty wavered. Sometimes the killing was poison or a dagger and tipped overboard in the night, but never a threat or a warning.

There were three men who had come with me from Black Hal's evil prison. John Flynn and Cal, born Esteban de Calvaro, had stood me true, but the other, Bal Tyler, had to be daggered and drowned. It was a good average when you know the nature of men as I do.

Cal appeared on deck, sporting a long velvet coat taken from the night's spoils. The red collar flattered his dark and handsome face.

Flynn glanced at him with a mocking look. "Señor Calvaro, ever the dandy."

Cal ignored him and pointed up at the flapping sails.

"You were right, mistress. The wind turned as we set foot on board. It still puzzles me how you always guess right, never fail."

"I told you, it's not a guessing game for me. I always knew the weather, even as a child. It's like a pricking on my skin or I dream it sometimes, or, like today, the pattern of clouds told me."

Cal crossed himself then grinned.

"Wherever it comes from, it's the greatest boon for a pirate queen and her men. You've kept us out of storms and dead seas and never suffered grounding or wreckage or even so much as a broken mast."

"The witch of the seas." Flynn tipped me a salute. "That's the rumour in every port."

Cal nodded gravely. "They say she made a pact with the spirits of the Deep, that she calls up wind and weather with a crook of her finger."

"Then aren't you lucky to be in her employ?" I laughed. "Queen Meg, like a mother to her crew. Far better than some old dog of a captain."

I knew what else they said about me, that I was barely out of girlhood, a beautiful woman, gorgeous in silk and lace and feathered and braided hair, a virgin maybe or with three men in her bed every night, who knew? But a prize, a jewel of the seas, who every other pirate captain coveted or feared.

And maybe not a witch, but certainly a heathen. The dim memory of Christian church on Sundays and holidays belonged to a past I had no further use for. If I worshipped anything, it was the Night Wing, the love of my life. I strode to the prow and slid my hand along the smooth weathered rail, my heart lifting at the perfect curve of timber against the dawn light.

From the first time I'd seen her, skimming light in the water, three masts straight and true, pricking the sunset clouds, I knew her as my freedom She was a home that would never be landlocked, my safe and perfect sanctuary. She was called the Princess then, but I named her as I saw her, Night Wing, diving like a hawk, disappearing like a ghost, a ship fit to carry Queen Meg on her voyages of plunder, adventure and revenge. I first sailed her to Marseilles where the port's finest shipwright fashioned and careened her. After that, Flynn, Cal and I scoured the coast gathering a crew I could trust or frighten into loyalty.

Between us we enlisted carpenter, surgeon and cook, and found the thirty five men and ten boys that made up the crew. All had been well until a few months before on Christmas Day. We had berthed near Plymouth. Twenty five men and boys went ashore and never came back. All were dead or kidnapped - at least, that's what Flynn heard when he went with a search party after the missing crew. He suspected Black Hal but, as far as I knew, that devil was still hiding in his sink hole at Honduras.

I took a long breath of the salt tang air. The loss had cut deep but I was a free woman, queen of my own ship and we were on a daring voyage. The plan was to intercept The Fair Lady merchant vessel on its return from Hispaniola to Spanish Main, taking a strange and circuitous route in the hope of evading pirates like us. I turned from the prow and walked back to Flynn who was still plying the wheel.

"You seem merry," he said, noting the spring in my step.

"I was thinking how you looked when you came back from the inn in Falmouth with rumours about the Fair Mary. Pleased with yourself, weren't you?"

"So I should be. Sniffed it out all by myself, then bribed the right man, threatened another – "

"And turned up at my cabin looking like you'd caught a fat rabbit for the pot."

"I have to give Jack some credit too," Flynn said, referring to Jack Lance, our small and portly navigator. "He plotted the crossing lines."

"But it was you that told us what we'd be crossing with – a wide bellied cargo vessel of only nine guns."

"I don't think Jack's recovered from how you kissed him on the cheek and danced a skip for us."

"It's a dancing business," I said. "Think of all the emeralds, silver and spices we'll be tipping through our fingers a week hence."

Suddenly the night's gruesome capture of the thieves seemed like naught but a faint memory.

"I'm off to sleep."

"Goodnight, mistress. No bad weather dreams, I trust."

CHAPTER 3

The dream wasn't about wind or weather but of a long hallway and glimpses of rooms where furniture was shrouded in white dust cloths. A tall mirror stood at the end of a passageway. I walked towards it. Waking with a start, I dragged the calico sheet from off my face. My mouth was dry, my breathing shallow. I let the rocking ship calm me, and thought of my cabin, curled like a shell inside the Night Wing's sturdy timbers.

I jumped off the bed to pour a beaker of water from the pewter jug that gleamed on the washstand. The water tipped cool down my throat, a benediction. Another couple of days at sea and water would be stale unless enough could be caught in the rain barrels. I pulled on my deep blue velvet robe and slid my feet into gold slippers decorated with parakeet feathers. They were part of the booty taken from a merchant ship we'd boarded near Malta a year ago. I never knew who the clothes belonged to but their owner couldn't have had more pleasure in them than I did. Garish finery was my insatiable weakness.

I glanced at a pile of books strewn across the table. This table, solid oak, was where I dined and read and perused the charts that Jack Lance drew up. A few of the bound leather volumes had slid to the floor. I bent to pick them up and heard a scraping noise outside the door. Crossing the cabin in a stride, I flung the door open, startling Pedlar before he could free a hand from the tray of food he carried. Pedlar's ruddy face deepened another shade of scarlet, making quite a picture with his flame red hair and green eyes. Pedlar was about twenty or so, near my own age, a yeoman's son who had lost his family in a terrible fire that wiped out half his village. Flynn had found him and he'd been a loyal crew member since.

"Beg pardon, mistress. There's some breakfast. I didn't want to wake you."

I thumbed a gesture for him to bring the tray inside and put it on the table. There was a platter with bread and cold chicken and a cup of fresh milk.

"Stanmore says to give you this, ma'am. He came across it in Looe."

He took a leather bound book from his jerkin and handed it to me.

"Found it, did he?" Stanmore acted the gentleman but was as light fingered as they come. I ran a finger down the embossed gold letters of the spine. "Plato's Republic. Greek philosophy in a fine leather binding. Can you read, Pedlar?"

His face took on a proud expression. "I can, ma'am. My brother learned off a clergyman and then taught me. He'd buy the Norwich Post when he could and ballads and there was always the Bible."

He gave me a nervous glance. I could read his thought as clearly as if he'd spoken it.

I laughed. "You won't find any bibles in a witch's lair."

Pedlar stood dumbly, the jest too close to the bone.

I patted his flinching arm. "But I dare say you can borrow a book now and then if you take care of it."

I smiled as he flushed red again. I knew he found me beautiful, as many men did. I released him with a nod and sat down to eat. The door scraped as Pedlar hurried out.

Selecting a piece of chicken off the platter, I popped it in my mouth. The meat was succulent, fresh pulled. I washed it down with a draft of water and leaned back in the chair, the better to feel the arching motion of the Night Wing as she cut steadily through the waves.

I stayed in my cabin, reading and making up for the past few nights' poor rest. The morning broke to a fine day. We would have a fair voyage and easy pickings at the end of it. The days rose and set beyond the gold tapestry curtains of my cabin, by candlelight and lantern light. Rainbows from the hanging crystals bounced on the counterpane and timbers.

One night, I dressed in yellow silk finery and joined the crew to dine below. Gower, a bear of a man but nicknamed 'Wolf,' sang one of the lewdest ditties I ever heard. One of the new men played a doleful air on the fiddle. It was so melancholy we all begged him for silence, and Stanmore feigned a stately jig in the narrow gap between the benches. It was a merry supper and afterwards I looked over the maps again with Jack Lance, reassured of our course.

It was one of the smoothest voyages I could remember, though cold, like ice at night, even with a wrapped stone to warm my feet and a thick pile of blankets to nest in.

CHAPTER 4

On the fifth day of our voyage, I felt it, like a squeezing on my neck. We were close. I peeled away my cocoon of bed linen then washed myself quickly in a basin of icy water.

"Sail!"

I heard the shout from above. My heart quickened. With hasty fingers I dressed to inspire the crew and myself. I donned a red silk gown with a wide feathered hat and a striped shawl of gold and green thread. I hooked my skirt in my belt, where cutlass and dagger lodged snug. My eyes were heavy rimmed with kohl. I left my lips as nature did, red and full and pouting enough to distract any men I had negotiation with though it was unlikely there would be parley today.

I had already discussed it with Cal and Flynn. The crew of the Fair Mary would surrender their cargo or go overboard, a simple fact. My brave costume was to cheer the men, lend an air of gaiety to the scene and remind them of their good life on Queen Meg's ship and the spoils she gave them, open-handed.

I opened my cabin door and, crouching under the low timbers, walked amidships. No one was below except the duty cook and a boy who was ill and coughing with the ague. He lay in his small hammock, white faced and miserable. His eyes widened as I paused beside him and patted his thin shoulder.

"Be of good cheer. You can help count the booty when we haul it on board."

I climbed the ladder and appeared above deck. The crew hallooed when they saw me, first my plumed hat, then my fine self.

"Does it get any better than this, boys?" I gave a grand gesture towards the Fair Mary's sail within our sights. "Our navigator, Jack Lance, has hit the mark!"

I strode to the fo'c'sle to stand behind Flynn as he ran the wheel between his expert hands. I was barely able to keep still for excitement.

"How are you, Quartermaster? A fine evening, I'd say."

Flynn grinned at me over his shoulder.

"Even better when we can turn south and get out of this ball-gripping cold."

"You were brought up soft for a peat bog Irishman."

Laughing, I drew my cutlass and raised it above my head. Every man's eye was on me.

"Go to it! Follow the bosun's word. As soon as we come up broadside, strike with iron shot and make haste with the grapplers before they have time to turn that slow wash-bin of a boat. They'll try a few cannon shot, but nothing to bother us!"

The crew listened, imaginations fired by my appearance. My voice, a good singing alto with 'lovely tone,' or so I'd often been told, spellbound them. With luck it would help them overlook the fact that some of the crew would die within the hour, that the deck would sluice with good men's blood and we would take other men's lives in plain sight of God, under the red ribboned sky.

The Mary had seen us coming too late and underestimated our speed, as many ships had before them, and glimpsed the flag only when it was past their time to manoeuvre beyond our sights. The Night Wing's crimson pinion with the emblem of the black bird of prey, wings at full spread, was enough to strike terror at the exact moment they needed to gather their wits.

"Night Wing!"

How many seamen on ambushed boats would cry that name, setting in train more legends and fear-stricken stories to work their quick poison. Most crews surrendered and I would order a handful killed on the spot. No negotiation, no mess. The rest would be stripped of all but the bare clothes they stood up in, and dumped off at the nearest port, wherever that happened to be. The same fate would be meted to Fair Mary.

The wind favoured us as we turned. The men readied the iron shot. With a good aim, it would rip the Mary's main mast. In the event, we dealt a perfect blow that rent down her sails and had her listing like a drunken slattern. The Night Wing dipped, a predatory bird, in for the kill. The hooks were flung across and we dragged our ship alongside. The Mary barely had time to fire three guns. The shot caused a scream and a scuffle on our deck. We rolled then righted and my men were swarming across, hand over hand on ropes. In moments, the Mary's crew abandoned ship, jumping overboard or scrambling below decks in terror for their lives.

It was hard to make out who was who in the fire and shadows. My eyes fixed on the Fair Mary's sails beating black and ragged like a wounded bird. I heard Stanmore yell. I could see his bulky frame as he braced the ropes for our men who still swarmed across to the Mary's listing deck. The wind picked up and turned, bringing the smell of blood and pitch on its salt tang.

"Sail!" The shout came from our boy on the crow's nest. "Sail to starboard!"

I whipped around but could see no sign of any other ship. Then it appeared, a black shape forming, three masts and square rigged. Without warning it bore down hard on us. More than half of our men were looting the Mary. Those left on board the Night Wing yelled warnings but the looters were slow and clumsy as they hefted booty from below decks, oblivious of the new danger.

The unknown ship fired, hitting us on the starboard. The Night Wing listed and bent her bow away from the Fair Mary. Ropes and grapple were wrenched free. I lost my footing and was thrown back against the hen cages, setting the birds a-squawking. In front of my eyes, two of my men were hurled into the sea as the rest heaved across the gap from the Mary, throwing boxes and bundles aside as they scrambled to take their places at the guns.

A fireball from the intruder ship arced in the night sky then came another. The Night Wing's flag caught ablaze. I raced to the port side and helped the men hack at the last of the ropes to tear us free from the cargo ship. I squashed my mounting panic. We had to run before this phantom ship had us. The night sky filled with billowing smoke made it impossible to make out the marauding vessel. I caught sight of little more than a swinging lantern and silhouettes bobbing like shadows on the ship's deck. Another volley of shots caught us broadside. My men, and boys, screamed and fell.

"All hands to the sails!" Cal shouted.

Hope of escape gave the men quick strength and soon the Night Wing was sailing fast and fleet before the wind, stricken, but out of the clutches of the unknown ship. As soon as we were out of range Flynn ordered a contingent of men to the oars to force the pace. I clung to the ship's wheel in his stead, grimly holding fast until Stanmore came to relieve me.

"We're out of it, mistress." His voice eddied in the wind that mercifully had us at our back. "Bosun says you're welcome to go below."

"The Night Wing will hold?"

"She'll hold."

CHAPTER 5

I ran below to my cabin, shaken to the core. The picture of the square rigger played over and over in my mind's eye. Where had it come from, and so fast? Fast as the Night Wing was, the ship had almost taken her. It was our damned carelessness and greed, all my men bent on plunder and no thought to watch our backs in case another looting ship appeared. I supposed that other spies apart from Flynn had found out about the Fair Mary's rich cargo. But the fact remained we had been attacked right there on the crossing line, as though we'd been followed.

In a heartbeat, I knew it, sure as daybreak. The unknown ship wasn't after the Mary's cargo, it was after the Night Wing. I strode two paces across the cabin and pulled back the window curtain. Oily black waves rolled by as we skimmed a fast pace west. I could feel her though, the list and roll, the jerking tremor. In spite of Cal's assurances, my Night Wing was a broken ship.

There was a knock at the cabin door.

"I'm not opening it."

"We're shipping water." Flynn's voice was muffled, his mouth to the lock. "Twelve dead, four wounded."

I clenched my hands into fists. "Get us to Scotland. I won't try to anchor where that ship could pick us off at any moment. We have to outrun them.'"

"We might not make it."

"Get us there, Master Flynn, all speed."

"On course as best we can, mistress, but there's more to tell you."

I threw the door open, alarmed afresh by Flynn's expression. His face was so carefully guarded that it revealed everything. I drew my shawl tight around my shoulders and sat down in my velvet covered chair, seeking comfort in its familiarity.

"If it's more bad news you'd better sit to tell me," I said.

Flynn took his place in the chair opposite. He was drained with weariness. The cords on his forehead stood out and there was a white edge to his lips. I pushed a bottle of madeira towards him. He poured a measure and took a couple of long swallows before speaking.

"Cal heard a rumour that the ship belongs to Black Hal."

The ship's timbers creaked in the silence that followed Flynn's remark then I was on my feet, shouting. "I don't like rumours and I don't need them." Memories of Black Hal, buried deep, broke loose. "Cal should know better. Why didn't he speak of it before?"

Flynn shrugged wearily. "He didn't pay it any credence, but when he got a look at that ship just now, it fitted what he'd heard exactly, the masts and rigging."

"I don't know how Cal could see anything out there. Besides, Hal would never have got off his knees after we stripped him of everything. How in damnation would he get a fast ship and a crew to do his bidding?"

"He ransomed a sultan's daughter, so they say. Made himself a fortune."

"A sultan's daughter? Don't make me laugh."

Flynn looked down at his beaker and took another swig. I couldn't meet his eyes. I stood up and lit candles, the soothing action distracting me from the dread that filled my bones. I, more than most, knew that Black Hal was an old sea dog of a survivor.

He'd once been wrecked, hanging on to a raft for four days. All the others, five men, drowned - but not him. He clung like the gnarly old barnacle he was, without sleep or food or drink, until a passing merchant ship picked him up, black from the sun and mad with thirst. The merchant's captain planned to get a price for his capture. Instead, half dead as Hal was, he ate and drank what they gave him then stole a boat, jumped ship in the night and escaped into Marseilles to surface a month later, the devil knows how, in Gibraltar.

"Black Hal," Flynn said. "There's talk he had a three-master fitted out in Honduras. Cal overheard a sailor say that Hal boasted he paid a witch to lay a charm on the ship so he could run after his daughter, Queen Meg."

The chill crept along my neck. I couldn't look at Flynn. His chair scraped on the timbers as he got to his feet. Suddenly, I wanted him gone.

"You should see to the men, not sit here swapping fishwives' stories."

"As you wish."

He was offended as I suppose he had the right to be. He'd brought me vital information and the cold in my bones whispered the truth of it but still I refused to believe it. In believing I would have to think about Hal, and with those thoughts would come memories sunk deep since the day I escaped him. Escaped and ruined him, I reminded myself. He could never have recovered from that, he was hated everywhere for his evil deeds, his betrayals and his unpaid debts. People like to make stories of ghosts and dead men. This tale was nothing more.

I refused to meet Flynn's eye as he left the cabin. He closed the door more roughly than was necessary, leaving me alone to face my own dark demons.

Harry Makepeace, Black Hal. I should have killed him, but even when I escaped him and had him at my mercy I couldn't touch him, the grip of fear on me was too strong. I had sworn to ruin him instead, and told myself it was a far worse fate that Hal's fortune and his ship were wiped away before his eyes. While we skirmished on a dock side in Marseilles, half of his men, bribed by me from gold I'd stolen out of Hal's own treasure, made mutiny. We set to butchering those that remained, killing twelve before the rest surrendered. The incident sealed my reputation once and for all. But still Hal lived, as by all accounts did his right hand man, Bloody Nick Rover, known by all as the General.

I knew where Hal's store of booty lay hidden and, almost four years from the day he'd taken me from my home, I sailed with a crew of men in a barque, low keeled to manage the shallows, to a sheltered bay of the Antilles. There, by torchlight, before dawn broke, we loaded every last doubloon of Black Hal's wealth. Then we disappeared. Again, I told myself it was worse for him that I'd left him alive to be the jest of pirates everywhere, but Hal turned even this to his own way. He boasted how he'd raised a daughter to be his pirate queen so that every prize and victory I won ever after reflected back to him as proof of his training of me.

Sometimes I even believed my own deception, that Black Hal, my captor and would-be 'father', had never ruined my life. I became Queen Meg, pirate queen, mistress of the oceans from old England to Barbary. I was a fable, a legend, beautiful, terrible, a crone, a maid, a woman of my own choosing. I rigged myself in the finest costumes, sometimes masked, sometimes painted, quick as death, lusted for and feared in equal measure. But where was Queen Meg now if Hal had maimed her ship?

The finery I had put on to cheer the men for the raid seemed like a mockery now. I dragged off the silks and plumage, exchanging them for man's pantaloons and a cambric shirt. I topped it off with a woollen shift and a dark blue robe. My face in the glass looked pinched and white. I etched more kohl around my eyes and tied a bandana of gay red and green around my head. My nose ran from the cold and unshed tears that ached in my throat, but I wouldn't let myself cry in fear of him, damn him to hell and back.

I scoured bread and stew off the platter. It was heavy in my mouth but I forced it down to take the strength and warmth of it. I washed it down with a measure of rum. The Night Wing listed and swayed more sharply than before.

I whispered to her as we ploughed through the waves. "Hold on. The wind is strong at our backs. Hold on, brave girl."

CHAPTER 6

We made it, reaching Scotland in a dawn that felt balmy after the freezing northern sea. Three miles off shore, the Night Wing rolling like a dying animal, we cast off the life boats. I had never abandoned my ship before, not once. I had to clench my fists not to lash out at Cal as he handed me into the first boat.

Jack Lance did his best to reassure me. "We'll tow her in safe, mistress."

I couldn't look at him. I couldn't look at my ship either, in case she made her death roll and capsized before my eyes.

Mist hung about the coastline as the row boats bumped into the shallows. The damp smell of moss and Scotland flooded my nostrils as I jumped waist deep into the freezing water. My skirts dragged like the arms of a dead man as we hauled our way through the rivulets of tide to stand at last on the white beach. Four boats crammed with men and boys drew in a bobbing line along the tide mark. Everyone straggled ashore to wait for my orders. I saw their eyes turn out to sea, to the Night Wing, but still I couldn't follow them.

I looked around at the men. They were silent and haggard with exhaustion after more than two days running full pelt from the attack, the terror of the unknown ship, Hal's ship, spurring us on. We'd outrun him or, more likely, he'd stayed behind to loot what was left of the Fair Mary. Either way, there was no sign of a black sail. Now we could disappear inland. I shivered with cold, my hands numb and feet sodden inside my boots.

Gulls keened overhead. Cal walked over to stand next to me.

"Stanmore knows the landlord at the Red Star Inn, up there in Stonehaven," he said. "I'll billet the men in a farmhouse and we'll all be wrapped round a warm breakfast soon as you like, ma'am."

"Not till she's safe," I muttered.

I couldn't avoid it any longer. I turned to look at her, surely not my Night Wing. There was a shape looming out of the mist, too low in the water, her masts half rigged, leaning sideways like a drunken doxy. It was all too plain, she was limp and broken. Turning on my heel I strode up the beach. Flynn caught up with me.

"You know she's done for."

I ignored him and walked on. His long pace easily caught up with my waterlogged footsteps.

"Best sell her for timber," he said. "Trade the booty from the Mary, get yourself a new ship." He put out a hand to halt me in my tracks. "I'll make sure your belongings are taken to the inn. We'll unload all the cargo that we can and I'll hire more men to keep guard for when the wrackers arrive to try to take their pickings."

My breath caught in a sob. This couldn't be, not the Night Wing, beached and broken, a target for that worst species of pirate, the shore wrackers that lured ships to the rocks with false signals and bonfires then looted them like carrion. I looked Flynn square in the face.

"I'm still mistress of this ship. The Night Wing will be repaired. Reckon up the spoils and find a shipwright."

I was at the Red Star Inn, hidden and holed up, for three days, while Cal and Flynn scoured the coast for a shipwright.

The waiting hadn't improved my temper, fed by bad dreams of Hal coming after us like a black spectre, while I walked barefoot and bereft of my ship like a ghost on the land, never to escape until death took me. I was as nervous as a cat. When the knock came I flung the door open so hard Cal jumped back, startled.

"Don't bother speaking unless it's to tell me she can be mended."

Cal quickly composed his proud features into their customary hood-eyed, supercilious expression. He smoothed his hands down the sides of his leather jerkin and announced,

"Your ship can be mended, ma'am. Luck brought us Joseph Conroy, the best shipwright on the eastern coast. He's here for business with his wife's uncle and we took him on board the Night Wing just now to make his assessment. Do you want to meet with him?"

"Just tell me what he said."

"Two, maybe three months and double the gold you have in your stores."

I hissed a breath. She could be saved, but I wouldn't last on land three months.

"Eight weeks to the day and he'll have his gold. Give him half now, half when it's done."

"And where is the other half to come from?"

"You do your business, Master Bosun, and keep your nose out of mine."

Cal put up a placating hand.

"As you say, ma'am, but I'm duty bound to warn you our Master shipwright is tough and seasoned and he won't stand to be cheated."

"No one is to be cheated."

Fir the first time in days, hope bubbled in my chest.

"The Night Wing will sail again, that's all that matters. I'll find him his gold. In the worst event we'll use the treasure stockpiled in Cartagena."

"But we'd need a ship to fetch it," Cal said.

"Why are you still crowding my chamber when you should be setting Mister Conroy to work?"

I slammed the door on him then ran to the window to catch a glimpse of where he was gone to meet the shipwright.

I was torn between relief that my ship could be saved and the hated feeling of being vulnerable to this unknown Mr

Conroy. I wouldn't meet him but I couldn't stay still either. Dressed in a dark robe, I made my way to the dry dock to stand behind the sea wall. The smell of seaweed and of tide turning made my heart leap after the stuffiness of the Red Star's rooms.

From my vantage point I watched Cal and Flynn walk to the beach. They joined another man who I assumed was Joseph Conroy, the man who was to save the Night Wing. He was tall and weathered with grey hair brushed back and tied in a black ribbon. I could see that Cal did most of the talking. Conroy pointed and gestured at my poor beached ship. I felt renewed shock at the sight of her. She was in dry dock, rolled half on her side, helpless and spent, exposing three gaping holes from the cannon shot.

I was too far off to hear their conversation but I heard voices raised and Conroy's gestures take a more aggressive tone. I assumed it was his response to being told he must mend the Night Wing in half the time and for half the money. Flynn stood unmoving while Cal gestured back. At last, Conroy reluctantly accepted the bag of gold Cal offered. My fingers gripped the cold edge of the wall as I saw him shake hands on the bargain. He would do it. There was hope for my darling ship.

The three men turned to walk slowly towards me. I ducked my head out of sight and hurried back to the inn. My heart beat with relief and excitement. I wasn't ready to go back inside where I had gone to ground for three long days and nights. I walked around to the stables and where I saw two horses grazing in the adjoining paddock. Another few steps took me around the side of the inn to the small garden behind. Hens flapped and clucked as I hurried up the small path to the rear door. One of the kitchen boys was leaning into the pig sty, scattering old vegetables in the trough.

"Is your master about?" I said.

He shook his head. I handed him a coin.

"When he returns, tell him I borrowed a horse."

CHAPTER 7

I rode along the coastal track to Stonehaven savouring the damp breeze, tang with sea salt. After the stifling prison of the inn and my anxiety that Night Wing was beyond repair, I felt a weight lifted from my mind. I was buzzing with anticipation, a sense of the tide turning back in my favour. I knew this feeling, my sixth sense, witch's instinct, call it what you will. Even on dry land I knew when there was a current worth following. My instincts pulled me along, in rhythm with the horse's canter and the swoop of sea birds to and fro their cliff-top nests.

After an hour or so I reached the first of the stone dwellings that led to the town's heart and the wide mouth of the port. Dismounting, I walked my horse half way down the hill and tethered it to a stone post. The horse snickered as I pulled a handful of grass and rubbed its damp coat. Leaning against the post, I watched as a barque glided into harbour and dropped anchor. A handful of townsfolk and a couple of customs men hung around the harbour wall to meet the sailors as they came ashore in their rowboats. I strolled down the hill. A couple of women who had been at portside approached and drew level. I hailed them.

"Where did the sailors come in from?"

One of the women looked me up and down.

"Bringing tin from Cornwall. Nothing fancy to buy if that's what you're after."

The other made a lewd gesture. "And if you're selling, you'd best be quick. The ones left ashore are running to the cathouse already."

I ignored the jest. I was seeking news, not money for favours. It was a cold and muddy day, the sailors that weren't seeking comfort in the brothel would surely need a sup. Keeping one eye on the straggling group of men, I made my way to the nearest ale house. Only one of the sailors carried on up the hill. I watched him stoop his head under the low eaves of the ale house door and enter. He was a rough looking character whose best days at sea were certainly over. I'd dealt with worse. I followed him inside.

The ale house fire was banked down to its embers. Beyond that, a muted shaft of light spilled through the dirty mullion windows.

I tapped the man on his shoulder. "Have a measure of rum on me," I said.

I handed a coin to the serving woman who slouched to the bar to fetch us a bottle and pewters.

The man glared at me."If I'd wanted a slattern, I'd have stayed down the street with the rest of the boys."

I replied as pleasantly as I could in the face of his surly manner. "I'm no doxy. I'm a merchant's wife, curious for news from any land beyond this godforsaken peat bog."

The serving woman clattered the tray and drinks on one of the four tables. I took a seat and gestured the seaman to join me. He sniffed as he sat down, nodded thanks, and tipped the drink back in one swallow. I lifted the jug to pour him another.

"You must have had a cold voyage."

The man grunted and swallowed down another measure.

"Come, sir, with my husband away, I'm starved of sea-faring conversation."

He coughed and spat towards the hearth. "We came from Plymouth. Raining a monsoon down there, blowing a gale near Hull town, and now like to freeze your balls in this northern mist. I hate Scotland."

I pushed another measure of rum towards him. Steam from his coat plumed in the warm fire lit air.

He called out to the serving woman. "I'll take a pie if you have one, or some cold cuts."

I noticed he didn't have the manners to offer me anything. We sat for a few minutes in silence except for the ticking of a mantel clock and the clatter of a knife and plate when the woman brought the food. The seaman ate like a dog. I felt as black-humoured as I ever had, sitting in that ale house with this dreg of a sailor, the evening light fading outside the narrow windows. Yet some instinct held me there.

He finished the last mouthful of pie and leaned back to pick his teeth. He nodded at me with a glance that was almost genial. "Picked up tin in Plymouth," he said. "They've a good method, those landowners. Instead of them bringing it to the docks one by one, they've made themselves a consortium. They hire a man to go round the estates and bring all the lode on a fleet of wagons. Half the time and twice the profit." He nodded approvingly.

I sat up. Perhaps this wagon train would be worth an ambush. "Do they do the same with other goods? Copper, for instance, or silver?"

"Can't say for sure. It was Lord Bartholomew Stede who started it and he's only got tin on his land. His son Daniel thought of the idea. Clever lad, I say. He's been in Europe these two years, due back in Cornwall in three weeks, special escort planned."

"Why an escort?"

"Daniel Stede is Lord Stede's only son and heir. Almost got kidnapped in Malta. They say the kidnappers could have named their price if one of them hadn't betrayed them all, hoping for the pickings himself."

The clock chimed six. I tapped a finger on the thick timber boards. An idea leapt into view, ripe as a peach and ready for picking. If a lord's son was worth kidnapping in Malta, he was surely worth a ransom in Plymouth.

"He returns in three weeks? To Plymouth?"

The man swilled the last of the rum, wiped his mouth on the back of his hand and nodded.

"Due to dock on the Star of Venus, three weeks tomorrow. Merchant rigger passage paid for in advance with gold coin, so they say. Captain's an ex-navy man, Taggart I think he's called."

The life of a pirate is built on such gems of information. I bit my lip to stop myself grinning like a child. The seaman placed his fat hand on top of mine. His fingers were still cold in spite of the fire and the free drink.

"So, you're looking for a bit of company while your man's away."

"Conversation only." I smiled, sliding my hand from under his. "My husband's fearsome jealous and prone to rage when the drink's in him."

The seaman sucked his tongue around his teeth as though considering some weighty matter. "You're a beauty, merchant's wife or no."

I got to my feet. "I'm tempted, of course." In a blue moon, I thought, glancing at his pot belly and mottled skin. I called to the serving woman. "Another rum!" Wagging my finger at the sailor, I said. "You finish your drink while I set off ahead. Don't want any scandal, do we?"

He winked conspiratorially as I practically ran from the ale house. I threw myself on the borrowed horse and galloped back to Stonehaven in the gathering dark. Plans for an ambush swirled in my mind and the feel of a gold coined ransom pricked my fingers. I would have the money for Conroy and a treasure besides.

CHAPTER 8

Flynn was waiting for me at the Red Star when I returned. His jaw sagged with relief when I walked into the parlour. The Red Star's landlord, Bar Sawyer, was with him. I nodded to them both.

"I need a good mulled wine and a plate of herring. Your horse is returned safe and sound, by the way. The stable lad's bedding him down. Flynn, share some supper with me, I have something to discuss."

I flung off my cloak and took a seat in one of the two easy chairs next to the fire. I noticed my boots were covered in mud, but that would have to wait. As soon as Sawyer was out of earshot, I gestured for Flynn to sit in the chair opposite.

"I have a plan, Mr Flynn."

"Good to see you in fine spirits again, mistress. Don't you want to hear how I bargaining went with Conroy?"

"I watched you from a distance. I could see he agreed, you sealed it with a handshake. Fine work, sir."

"He agreed most reluctantly. I hope you have the ready payment when we come to collect the ship. I wouldn't answer to his actions if we go back on our word."

I waved aside his caution. "Like I said, I have a plan."

A serving boy arrived with the supper tray. He poured wine for me and Flynn while I took a few mouthfuls of fish and bread. As soon as the door closed behind him I leaned forward, keeping my voice low.

"Me, you, and six of our best men ride south, day after tomorrow."

Flynn frowned.

"What lies south that requires such haste? Does it have anything to do with where you disappeared for half a day without a word?"

"I was suffocating in that room upstairs so I went for a ride to Stonehaven to see what news from the outside world. I picked up a very tasty morsel from a sailor just come from Plymouth."

I took a mouthful of wine then raised the cup in salute.

"The Lord of Stede's son docks in Plymouth in three weeks after a time overseas. With a good pace, we'll be positioned and ready to play highwaymen when he takes the road home."

Flynn sat up in his chair. "Stede? I've heard he's one of the wealthiest landowners in North Cornwall. I take it the young lord is bringing a fortune back with him?"

"He is the fortune - at least, he will be when Stede coughs up a ransom. His hide will more than cover my debt to Mr Conroy."

Flynn pursed his mouth in a way I knew, ready to play the cautious counsel.

"Beg pardon, but where's the surety in that? Stealing ready money is a good gamble but a kidnap ransom? Stede's not bound to agree and even if he does, negotiations take time, time that we don't have if we are to honour our bargain with the shipwright."

"His only son and heir taken by pirates? Stede will pay in a flash. Now, fInish your drink and go muster the raiding party."

Reluctantly, Flynn got to his feet.

"Are six men necessary? That's a lot of horses, and you could as easily hire a few stalwart sailors in Plymouth."

"Cutthroats more like. I'm not taking any chances. It'll be six men of the Night Wing with their own livelihood at stake to back up their loyalty to me."

Flynn shook his head.

I fished out a ring that was hung on one of the pendants around my neck. It was pink gold and encrusted with diamonds.

"Here, you'll need money to kit the horses."

Flynn frowned. "That's your talisman ring. Your own booty from the Night Wing's first raid."

"It's well spent if it gets my ship back on water again. Trust me Flynn, I feel this sure as I feel a weather or tide change."

He shook his head then grinned.

"Plymouth it is."

I felt nothing but relief to get away from Stonehaven. Besides, I had a task now, a pirate's adventure. It was nothing to compare with ambushing a ship after a chase on the high seas. Still, boarding a carriage and kidnapping a lord – that would do nicely for now.

I had never lost a raid before the bungle with the Fair Mary and I needed to prove to myself I was still invincible. Cal had reassured me that one loss in four years is forgivable, but he was wrong. To lose even once was the thin end of the wedge for a pirate queen. News of it could give other pirates the notion that they too could catch the Night Wing, blow a hole in her side and frighten her from the oceans.

I was glad that one of the men Flynn picked for our party was Stanmore. He was a loyal seaman who had been with the Night Wing for two years, affable and strong as an ox. It was he Flynn sent to knock on my door at four o' the clock two mornings after to tell me the men were ready and waiting in the stable yard. I was already wide awake and dressed. My bag had been packed the night before so it only remained to thrust musket, sword and dagger in my belt and stow three bags of coins in my tunic pockets. The money was change from the sale of the diamond ring after Flynn had paid for our expedition's expenses.

I blew out the candle and ran downstairs without a backward glance. Flynn and the others of our raiding party huddled in the damp yard with just the light of a storm lantern to pick out their shapes against the dark wall. Bar Sawyer was still abed but his cook was up to serve us mulled wine and oat cakes. I could barely grip the wooden beaker, my hands were so cold, even in my thick riding gloves. The spiced wine scalded my throat but loosened my limbs of their morning cramp.

I glanced around the men's shadowy faces to check who was with us. Young, red-haired Pedlar, then Hugh Catter, who always looked as fresh as a daisy flower next to the other seamen, and Gower, with his shaggy hair and rough temper, and Joshua, an ex-poacher who I'd saved from hanging. Like the others, he owed me a debt and gave his loyalty to serve Queen Meg. Only Cameron, the last of our party, had come to seafaring as a true vocation when he was a boy of ten. He had sought out the Night Wing for her prowess on the seas. Sometimes known as Old Man Cam because of his serious demeanour and grey hair, he was still a few years shy of thirty. Cal and Jack Lance were to stay behind to keep an eye on the shipwright and the rest of the seamen who were billeted at the farm to await our return.

Gower lifted his head and sniffed the air. "Dawn breaking."

It promised to be a clear morning and no mist to cover our departure so we readied ourselves without delay. Wrapping our cloaks tight against the sharp cold, we led the horses, their hooves muffled in sack cloth, on the back road out of the village. We reached the crest of the hill before cock crow. I leapt up in the saddle and the men followed suit. I set the pace at a canter along the moorland road.

CHAPTER 9

At mid-morning we turned west and inland to skirt the Firths of Tay and Forth. By now we had settled into a steady trotting pace. The climbing sun warmed the air. Stanmore drew alongside at the front of the group.

"A fine morning after all, ma'am."

"And good to be on the move, even if it's the saddle rather than on deck."

"I'm sorry about the Night Wing, mistress. She's been a home to me these past two years, and saved me from a prison cell."

"Or a knifing, more like. The husband of the girl you'd been canoodling with came after you and he had murder in his soul if ever I saw it." I laughed. " I hope she was worth it."

"I'm a reprobate dog, I know it, but you gave me safe exit on the Night Wing just the same." Stanmore smiled slyly. "I wouldn't pick any woman over you, ma'am. Unless it was the Night Wing herself."

"I'm nobody's woman."

"I hear different, begging your pardon, ma'am," Stanmore said, trying to keep the joke going. "There's men courting you in droves."

"Pirates, you mean, bidding in the hopes of adding me to their dynasty. Robber barons promising a place for me in their halls."

My mood turned sour as I remembered how Black Hal had used me. His scheme was always to promise the goods - me - but not to hand them over until he had gained the best price possible. After that he made an excuse to withdraw so he could auction the prize all over again. That's how he'd sold me as a virgin five times over.

"The trick is in leading them on," I said. "Accept the gifts, consider their courtship, their offer of this or that nephew, perhaps even become betrothed. There's always a way to wriggle out of it at the last minute. Unfaithfulness is easy to prove, especially where men are concerned." I heard my voice turn more bitter as I spoke. "Most men can be tempted by a handpicked doxy, even on the night before their wedding. And most certainly when they think they won't be found out. I even killed a man for betraying me, though I had set the trap myself. I had to protect my name, didn't I? Though I made sure I kept the chest of jewels and finery his rich buccaneer uncle had given me as dowry."

I flipped my hand and rolled my eyes coquettishly, making Stanmore laugh, and to change the mood. The story had been told over but it did no harm to remind them of Queen Meg's deadly cunning.

As night fell, we paid for rooms at a gentleman farmer's house. Hugh Catter, being the most well-spoken of the crew, went ahead to fix it and managed the business well enough for no questions to be asked or for me to be introduced. We were well rested and fed that night but the heavy rain that poured all next day and the one after put an ill humour on our spirits.

A seafaring life makes you accustomed to exposure to the elements and the constant damp on board that seeps into everything. On squally days the deck is awash, and a sea fog can drench you as thoroughly as a storm. But on land you should at least have the luxury of dry shelter and a warm fire. There was no shelter for us as we negotiated the road south. We had to press on in fear that the way would bog and slow our journey. I had no intention of turning up too late for the Star of Venus when she docked at Plymouth with her lucrative cargo: Item, one lord's son of good inheritance.

The weather cleared on the fourth day as we drew south of the Roman Wall. The afternoon sun that struggled through the clouds wasn't strong enough to dry our travelling clothes, but it was a welcome sight. Pedlar, who we prized on board for his fine voice, sang shanties and ditties and Gower told us a long story of the Maid of Ronan whose mother had been a mermaid and whose father was a swarthy king of the Orient. The Maid had inherited the worst of both their looks and couldn't get a husband. Even the king despaired, in spite of all his fortune and threats, until one day a fair horseman rode into the city and offered his hand.

"I have no lands or fortune," Gower said. He made us laugh by mimicking his idea of a nobleman's voice. "Neither do I crave them, but I would marry this maid because she appeared to me in a dream and a wise man told me that good luck would follow us both until the end of our days if we be wed."

On their wedding night, with many jests pertaining to her mermaid's tail, the marriage was consummated. Lo and behold, the swarthy maid became fair and her tail disappeared, to be replaced by two fine white legs. They lived happily after, spawning two sons and two daughters, though the youngest sported a fish tail and ebony complexion.

I laughed with the rest but felt a tear at the part where the horseman professes his love. That will never be me, I thought. Black Hal had told me what I was and I could never shake it from my mind. 'Damaged cargo, Meg. You're booty, and a spiteful bitch after my own heart who'll shrivel any man who gets close enough.'

I wished I didn't believe him. More than that, I wished he didn't haunt my thoughts since the attack at sea. The idea of Hal in possession of a fast boat and fresh crew unnerved me more every day. Worse, the bad dreams began halfway through our journey and the memories they brought seeped into my thoughts on the long days of riding.

Margaret Robertson. I never thought of her these days, the girl I'd been before the pirates came, but now she picked at my mind like a lost spirit. That girl had a father and mother, two fine horses, a fencing master and a library full of books. The raids had come and gone along our Cornish coast, but we were safe, we thought, a good few miles from the ocean. We had suffered thieves, what grand house doesn't? But my father had his loyal men about him, John Timmins and the farm hands, our bailiff, and the blacksmith, Will, who could stand up to anyone. But they hadn't reckoned on thirty pirates, armed to the teeth, creeping inland, rich pickings on their mind. The pirates were led by Black Hal, the most ruthless cutthroat to sail out of Hispaniola and his Caribbean hideout, bent on stealing from the English landowners.

Black Hal, or Harry Makepeace as he'd been christened, had been a pirate since he was forced from his humble farm inheritance by bad crops and debt. He was reborn as Black Hal, or 'Firestick Harry' after the lighted grappling hooks he used to capture ships. What can I tell you of him? A nasty, small man, weathered by endless voyages, cut by sea battles, mean-faced at the hand life had dealt him. 'I'm your father now,' he told me in the first minutes after he took me from the house. I stood with him gripping my wrists, alongside his vicious first mate 'General' Boyet, and watched the house burn, and my parents inside it. I remembered little after, only a dull ache and blackness, the crack of sails and weeks at sea. I was just fourteen.

'I'm your father and brother and husband and all now.'

He smiled and gloated, but he didn't take me, not then. He had a higher prize in mind. I was dressed and paraded in one port then another until word got out that Black Hal had a fine virgin daughter to sell to the highest bidder. It was in those months I learned how you could become someone else, change your looks to whatever you cared to invent and people would believe what you told them. I even learned to believe it myself, a good plan when you wished yourself dead and far from Hal's evil grasp.

The bidding went up and up. It was a year before Black Hal gave me over to an earl for a sack of doubloons. A day later the earl was dead, a mysterious dagger through his guts, while I was kidnapped back again and taught the pretence of still possessing a maidenhead. The earl never consummated his bargain, or so the story went out, and my price stayed high.

The next man who took me died three days after, and so began my reputation as a death sprite. The bidding after that was from men who fancied the challenge. I killed the next one myself, my precocious skills with dagger and rapier honed by my new life as a pirate's daughter.

But after Hal and his cronies passed me around like a slattern, I had never let a man near me. I'm not saying I was never tempted but I count it a point in my favour and revenge on Hal that I could walk away from even the prettiest man without a backward glance.

"Mistress?" Pedlar's voice broke my reverie. My horse had fallen back from the others by twenty yards. Pedlar was turned in his saddle, looking back at me.

I called to him. "I thought my horse had lost a shoe but all's well."

CHAPTER 10

We made Plymouth with two days to spare. Flynn, Pedlar and Stanmore spent their time at the docks, finding out where the Star of Venus was due to berth, who was the captain, how many crew and if there were privateers on board. Joshua planted himself in the dockside tavern and, by plying the right man with drink at the right time, discovered the our target wasn't to be met by his father, Lord Stede. A coach and four soldiers were commissioned to take him first to Looe, God knows why, then north to Wadebridge and onward to his father's estate.

We redesigned our plan accordingly. We would let him disembark, spend a comfortable night in Plymouth lodgings and make his errand in Looe. No doubt a messenger would be sent to Lord Stede to let him know his son was safe and setting off for home. As soon as that despatch went ahead, we would make our move and take young Daniel. Stede would think the delay in his son's arrival home was caused by weather or road. It would buy us a day at least before he bothered to send out a search party. By then we would be far off, dipping night oars from Plymouth to Brittany on the barque that Hugh Catter was just now hiring with the last of our coin.

Flynn had already sent word to a trusted man who would give us refuge on the French coast where we could hide out a few days with our kidnapped prisoner. Meanwhile, Cam would ride north with a ransom note. With luck we would be counting a gold coin ransom soon after.

The next morning I was as excited as if it were Christmas Day. Soon, soon, the Night Wing would be good as new, I'd pay off the shipwright and we'd be gone on wind and tide directly.

The Star of Venus, a wide bellied three masted galleon, showed a fine sail as she slid into Plymouth port at ten o'the clock. I was glad we didn't have to snatch our target dockside. The place was swarming with privateers on guard duty for the wine and spices the galleon carried in its hold. My fingers itched to steal it but we had to keep our eyes on the main prize.

I spoke to Cameron before he set off with Gower and Stanmore to act as spies. "If we play him right, Lord Stede will afford us the cargo prize three fold to have his precious son back with him and all limbs intact."

I was too likely to be recognised so I stayed in my room all day. Joshua was nervous with so many militia about so he skulked at the tavern where he and the others had their lodgings. Flynn, acting as go between, promised he'd let me know as soon as there was news. The clock was chiming four in the afternoon before I heard his knock on my door, three taps then one loud rap, as we had arranged. I let him in.

"Stede's boy safely stowed, m'lady."

I clapped my hands.

"Some of Venus' crew escorted him to lodgings near Customs House, privateers and their bayonets around him like porcupine's quills."

"We'll give them a fair start tomorrow then follow them to Looe." Flynn nodded as I went over our plan once more. "We'll ride clear of the town perimeter, two miles at least, before we set our ambush. It means one night sleeping out in the moors, but it can't be helped. Did you purchase everything we need?"

"I have tent cloth and a prayer for fine weather. We'll be ready and waiting when the coach takes the road north again the next day."

"Unless he decides to stay another night in Looe." I strode to the window and back again, restless as a kitten. "What the devil is his business there anyway?"

"He has an aunt living there, his mother's only sister."

I rolled my eyes.

"How very affectionate. You would think his father had waited long enough to greet him – two years in Venice and Antwerp, wasn't it?"

"And Malta, finishing his education, I heard. He's been trained in banking and trading. They say the boy was too fond of the land for his father's liking. Lord Stede wants him to be more hard-headed about what the land is worth, how it can prosper him, not be a milksop for peasants to take advantage of."

I laughed. "I dare say we'll round off his lessons nicely. Commerce the pirate's way."

We shared a flagon and an early supper then Flynn left for the tavern and the doxy he'd been promising himself since we arrived. A girl in every port was Flynn's mission, motto and rule to live by. He had a wife somewhere, or so he once told me in his cups. Cal assured me it was two wives at least.

The next morning we rode out of Plymouth town a bare mile behind Stede's hired carriage and escort. We counted four armed privateers, two in front and two behind, close guarding the carriage's passenger. I noted with satisfaction the escort must have cost a pretty penny. Stede's extravagance boded well for the high ransom I could wring out of him.

The day fell overcast and the air oppressive under the low banked cloud. Lord Daniel's carriage was slow as a funeral cart. Pedlar acted as scout, riding ahead to check the carriage's progress. As the day dragged on and we neared Looe, we pulled off the road to seek a place to camp, ready for our ambush the next day. I was still aggravated by Stede's delay in setting off on the road home.

"What if he stays in Looe a week? He must have secret business he doesn't want his father to know about, a gaming circle or a special whore he's been saving up."

"Our spy said he's visiting the aunt, no more," Flynn said. "He has to travel north directly. It makes no sense for his father to retain an armed escort for days on end."

While Joshua bagged wild rabbit for supper and the other men set up camp, I stayed my patience by mentally counting the ransom money and imagining my next meeting with Conroy. I couldn't wait to hand him the bag of gold and take back the Night Wing, hopefully fully mended. Then we would sail, by God we would. It was freedom I craved, not a night of huddling under tent cloth in the middle of a dank moor.

Dusk crept in with a thunder-filled sky that thankfully never broke, though we saw lightning flashes near the coast. I failed to sleep more than a few fitful dozes. I was wrapped in three blankets but still cold. The smell of dark earth hung in my mouth and nostrils. Each time I dozed, I was haunted by a fancy of seeing Hal's ship, the Hell's Mouth, as though it could sail, black flag fluttering, clear across the rolling moors.

At first light, Pedlar returned from his scouting expedition in Looe. He pulled his wide hat from his head and rubbed a hand through his damp red hair. "The aunt lives in a modest house, south of the town. There's no husband but there is a daughter and four servants - "

"I don't care how many servants or daughters. Is the young lord on his way?"

"The groomsmen were preparing the carriage when I poked my nose around the stables. They were leisurely about it but Stede's son is leaving by noon at the latest for Wadebridge."

I clapped him on the shoulder.

"Thank God! Flynn, get the men ready. We have some dry land buccaneering to do."

Everything was clicking into place like the parts of a well-oiled clock. We broke camp and moved close to the road. Gower and Joshua took the horses a quarter mile off. There, they made a small campfire and sat huddled in their great cloaks, looking for all the world like a couple of gypsies. The remains of an old stone wall formed a makeshift hiding place for the rest of us.

There was little traffic on the road, a couple of riders and a farmer with a cow tethered to his cart. They barely gave Joshua and Gower a passing glance. At mid-morning, the carriage appeared, bowling along at a smart pace. A startled hare dived across the road in front of them. The four privateers were in place, two in front and two behind. The driver sat alone on top. Stede was presumably alone and snug inside. We burrowed down and waited until they passed.

I nudged Pedlar to signal Gower and Joshua to make haste with our horses. We led them at a trot then mounted and made a swift canter to overtake the carriage. Dry open moorland is easy terrain when you're accustomed to a deck blowing shot all around you and the pitching sea threatening to cast you overboard at any moment. We acted, fast and deadly. The men took the two rear privateers with barely a whisper. Me and Gower went for the two front riders. I had mine on the ground in a flash but Gower made a bad job of it and caught a shoulder wound from the privateer's sword.

The driver had thrown up his arms in surrender at the first glimpse of us. Flynn leapt up beside him and brought the carriage to a rumbling halt. Pedlar and Cam guarded the doors while we bound the prisoners' hands and feet and herded them in to the roadside ditch.

I heard a sudden curse from Pedlar. "Dammee, there's another in the carriage."

I swung around to see a musket and the sleeve of a black coat poking out the carriage window. The man fired the weapon, clipping Cameron badly enough in the thigh to lame him. I wrenched open the door and had the man at sword point while the powder was still cupped in his hand to reload. He looked like a clerk or some such. Beside him was a tall young man, obviously a gentleman, unarmed. That he was unsettlingly handsome took me completely by surprise.

Suddenly, young Daniel was more than faceless booty, a sack of spoils to barter for my ship's restoration. God help me, the clerk almost got past my blade, and lunged at me with the musket. Stanmore fell on him just in time. Daniel threw his arm across the clerk to protect him.

"It's me you want, leave him be!"

I pointed at the clerk with my rapier. He whimpered.

"Tie him with the others," I said. "Take them off the road, out of sight."

"You're a woman," Daniel said. He sounded incredulous.

I was wearing man's garb with a hooded cloak so Daniel must have thought me a highwayman. He looked as shocked by my appearance as I was by his. I took in his classic features, broad shoulders, fine jaw atop an elegant neck. I stared him down. I was pirate Queen Meg and the ambush had succeeded.

"You've never seen a woman handle a sword or command fighting men?" I said. "Joshua, tie Lord Stede's hands and ride with him in the carriage. Gower, Cameron! Get in the carriage too and see to your wounds. It's time to be away."

CHAPTER 11

Before the ambush, I had planned to ride in the carriage and find out more about Daniel and his father. Now, that was out of the question. I was taken aback at my reaction to Daniel and I didn't trust myself to be as ruthless or impartial as I needed to be. At the same time I refused to think myself smitten at the mere sight of a handsome face.

Joshua, Gower and Cameron took their places inside the carriage. Pedlar took the place of the driver and we set off at a fast pace west, the privateer's horses harnessed behind. The sooner we were off English soil the better, as far as I was concerned. All the way to Plymouth, my thoughts jumped like hares, first on the ransom money that I would soon be pulling out of Lord Stede's pockets, the next on a pair of blue eyes set in a face more comely than any man's had a right to be.

To distract myself, I went over the plan again. Across the Channel we would be safe at my friend Lennox's house. There we would wait for a response from Lord Stede to the ransom letter Hugh Catter was to deliver. As soon as Stede promised me what I asked for, I would send word for him to meet us in Plymouth with the gold. When he handed over the ransom he would be told Daniel was waiting for him in Dover. By the time he made the journey and reunited with his son, we would be well on the way to Scotland and the Night Wing.

At last we reached Plymouth and, in spite of the road becoming busier with every mile, no one challenged us as we brought the carriage around to the edge of town. Blessing our lucky stars, we dismounted and unloaded the carriage, or rather the men did. I kept clear of our prisoner, though he was gagged and hooded. Flynn had the carriage contents brought with us, including a box of coin that proved an unexpected bonus. He sent Joshua in to town to purchase grog and liniment for Cameron and Gower's wounds.

Stanmore, still in privateer's guise, stowed the carriage at the rear of the warehouses. Flynn took charge of Daniel. I beckoned Hugh Catter over and gave him his instructions.

"Take the horses and get what you can for them. Give us one day's start then hightail it north to Lord Stede and deliver him this."

I drew a sealed letter from inside my jerkin and handed him the thick, crackling parchment. His brown eyes narrowed.

"I won't let you down, m'lady."

"I know you won't. Keep yourself safe and at a distance. We don't want Stede springing you in a trap."

Catter smiled and bowed a courteous farewell.

I smiled back then an odd feeling overtook me. I'd always thought Catter the best looking of men. Now, the only face I could see was Daniel's. I grimaced, crushing the thought. I stayed to watch Catter mount his horse and lead the others trotting way, my ransom demand to Lord Stede stowed inside his coat.

The rest of us made our way to the docks where Flynn had arranged to meet our hired boat. There were no vessels anywhere along the slime-covered walls and slipways. The place stank like Neptune's grave.

"We made good time," Flynn said. "They'll be here with the boat presently."

While we waited, Joshua returned with provisions and we ate an impromptu picnic. Flynn jumped to his feet.

"The barque's here," he said.

The boat that anchored in the south corner of the harbour was a rough looking vessel, nothing to attract attention. I saw the captain knew what he was about, turning the boat neatly and ready for the tide. A row boat skimmed out to fetch us, the shifting current slopping messily under its bows. We crushed on board under the glare of an evil-eyed seaman who plied the oars.

"Only three crew and us," Flynn said. "I kept it discreet, as you asked. This is Jed, part owner."

Jed glared some more and spat over the bow as he expertly pulled us in alongside the barque.

"The Starfish," he announced in a rough Breton accent. "Pretty name, eh?"

One of his crew gave me a hand on board as I clambered up the matted rope ladder. As soon as I stepped on the barque's timbers I could feel the pull of the tide. A sea fret was on its way. The captain must have felt it As soon as we were all aboard, the barque pulled anchor and we hastily set off.

Within minutes, the fret was on us. It turned to a squall that had us bouncing and keeling a clumsy exit through the harbour mouth.

It was a bad crossing, the deck washed by one heavy shower after another. I stayed above for most of it to feel the cold air and spray. The fresh blow of the wind was intoxicating after the days of tension leading to the kidnap. Now I could let it sink in that my plan had succeeded. The ransom would soon be mine. I could have danced a jig. As if on cue, Cameron, who had been well dosed with grog while Joshua dressed his injury, set up a wailing song.

"Maids a plenty, treasure's empty,
Fill the pot and steer me way, boys…"

Gower climbed up on deck to hand me a tot of rum and a welcome plate of oatcake and cured fish.

"You seem recovered," I said.

He tapped his bandaged shoulder. "I've had worse, ma'am. Cam is suffering a bit with his leg, though." We heard Cameron set off on another raucous ditty. "Sorry about the noise below. We may have given him a mite too much rum to ease the pain."

I threw back my own drink and grimaced.

"He must be merry to drink a quart of this dog piss."

Flynn suddenly appeared from below, dragging Daniel with him. I glared at him.

"Why in hell's name have you brought him up on deck?"

"He's been sick as a wench, m'lady. I don't know how he made the crossing from Italy. Says he had a remedy for it and the ship was steadier."

"He's a milksop lord's son. What can you expect?"

"So we won't press gang him to the Night Wing?"

I was annoyed by his sidelong glance. He'd noticed my fancy for the young man.

"Why? Are you hoping I'll stay my rule about no whores on board so you can pick up a brace of them along the coast?"

My rough talk deflected the conversation. Everyone chimed in with their own 'Flynn and the whore' story, the red haired one in Southampton, the twin sisters in Madeira.

Daniel shouted over our laughter. "I demand you turn back!"

We all turned to look at him. He gathered himself to say more but instead lurched to the boat's side and threw up in the sea.

Stanmore laughed. "Looks like the current will take your dinner home before you."

I took a step towards Daniel and raised my voice above the blustering wind. "Demand isn't a word I like to hear, unless I'm the one saying it."

Daniel wiped his mouth and glared back at me.

"Who are you? Your men call you Queen Meg but you're no older than I am. Is your father or husband some foul pirate, too?"

I was so used to dealing with men who never questioned what I bid them that I was taken aback by Daniel's insult. Worse, I felt how I wanted to drink him in, how I let the words hang between us instead of mastering the situation.

"Take him below! I don't care if his lordship spews his guts the whole voyage."

"Who's to look after him?" Gower said.

"You are."

I turned my back squarely on them and went to talk to Jed about our route, though with his surly manner and poor English, it was an one-sided conversation

CHAPTER 12

Three days later, in the early hours of a wet morning, we reached the Breton coast.

"We need Jack Lance for a job like this," Flynn said under his breath.

The barque's captain turned the boat across current, looking in vain for our destination, a deep cove with a long line of jutting rock that led the way to Lennox's house.

Stanmore leaned over the side, peering into the blackness. "You can't see a brace of pigs out there, never mind a hidden cove."

The captain paced across the deck once then called to Jed. "Weigh anchor!"

There was a scrape of rope, a pause then the deep splash that told us we were land bound again. Suddenly we saw them, two bobbing pinpricks of light, dancing against the pitch black mass of coastline. Joshua ran below and brought a lantern. Holding it aloft, he swung it, once, twice, then covered the flame. On shore, one lantern dowsed but the other copied our two blinks.

I let out a sigh of relief. Lennox had received our message. Jed and two of our men dropped the row boat and we scrambled into it and made our way to shore. The oars dipped in the ghostly water as we kept eyes fixed on the small light leading the way to our haven and hideout.

The men struggled to bring the row boat close in and we bumped and scraped our way along the foot of the low but sheer cliffs until we found a landing place. Even so, we had to plunge waist deep and wade to shore. After that, it was a waterlogged trudge up the coast path and along the ridge to Lennox's house. Rain splashed down as we straggled along. Joshua dragged the bound and hooded Daniel while Gower helped Cameron, silent after his carouse and slowed by his wounded leg. Flynn had gone back in the boat to fetch our boxes and to help the seamen bring the barque closer in.

The long, low range of the house stood at the crest of the rise. It was a substantial building set in twenty acres or more. Lennox was nowhere to be seen but the door stood open, its rosy-lit interior like a treasure cave in the sleet-ridden dark. I went in ahead and almost collided with a servant at the entrance then laughed as I saw Lennox walk down the stairs to greet us. Ever the dandy, he wore an embroidered cambric robe and a blue shawl over his nightshirt.

Lennox had been handsome in his day but good living had added flesh and marked his face an unattractive shade of red. He spread his arms to greet me then kissed me on both cheeks.

"I thought you'd missed the tide."

"Caught the tide but missed the cove. Thank God for your lanterns."

"You see I remembered the old signal for smuggling." Looking pleased with himself, he gestured towards the stairs. "We have four rooms made up, two beds apiece, not counting your own. The rest will have to make do with the barn."

"The rooms will suffice. It's a small crew, as my message told you."

Lennox nodded. "You have your old guest room at the top of the stairs. There's supper and a fire lit."

"Then I won't need escorting. Go back to bed, Lennox. We'll talk in the morning."

"Perhaps a word, in my sitting room?"

"Can't it wait?"

Lennox shook his head and walked ahead of me to a room at the far end of the passage.

I heard Joshua mutter something behind me, then more clearly. "Can we trust this gentleman farmer or whatever he calls himself. He sounds more Irish than Breton to me and you can't help wonder how he came by such a fine house?"

I turned to him. "I'll forgive you that, as you never met with Lennox before this. It's a long tale, but the heart of it is that Lennox owes me for this house. He trades all along this coast, if you call smuggling trade, and he's well-guarded by handpicked men. Best of all, he'll hear rumours of any snoopers or spies well before they can catch us."

I looked past him to the others gathered in the passageway.

"Gower, I want you to share a room with the prisoner. Keep his hands bound and call at once if there's anything amiss."

Gower nodded reluctantly and went outside to fetch Daniel. I took off my wet cloak and went to join Lennox. The sitting room was as I remembered. There were embroidered cushions on the couches, a polished wood table laden with bottles and a wall of books, most of them unread. Lennox's mind ran more to spying and trading than literature.

He poured me a glass of rum and took one for himself. "It appears you have a prisoner. May I enquire as to his crime?"

"Wealth. I won't tell you his name. Suffice it to say a message is on its way to an interested party. We should have news in the next day or two."

"Ransom, is it?" Lennox nodded appreciatively then his expression turned serious. "I should tell you there are rumours your ship is broken."

"I don't know who told you but I'll have his tongue if he broadcasts it."

Lennox held my gaze. "Is it true? I've heard there's more than one pirate plotting to find your ship and destroy it once and for all. Then go after Queen Meg herself."

I felt chilled with dread. Night Wing had to be safe, Cal would oversee Conroy and make sure of it.

"Is it true?" Lennox said.

"Far from it. Some of my crew came with me on a land venture, too lucrative to miss. Perhaps that's why there were rumours of my ship being out of action."

Lennox nodded, but I knew he wasn't convinced.

"If there are rumours being peddled, I'd like you to spread a few more for me. Put it out among your spies that the Night Wing has been sighted in every port from Venice to the Spanish Main."

Lennox opened his mouth to reply but just then Gower walked in with Daniel. The cloak and gag were gone and I was undone all over again, staring at him as if I was a kicked

mule. His eyes looked darker in the fire lit room. I couldn't
take my own gaze off them, and when I did it was only to
stare at his mouth then back to his long fingered hands that
twisted a ring around one knuckle. I managed to break the
moment.

"Why have you brought him in here? Lennox doesn't need to
be implicated. Take him upstairs and out of sight."

"The fire's not lit and we're soaked through."

Lennox put down his glass and took a step to the door. "I'll
see to it, and have supper fetched." He glanced at me and
smiled. "Don't worry, mistress, I'll attend to the other matter
we spoke of. And I'll make sure no one in the house catches
sight of your fine looking guest."

He bowed and gave me a knowing, vulgar look that sat ill on
his round red face. I turned on my heel and left, making a
poor show of seeming indifferent.

I climbed the stairs, my footsteps heavy in my water-logged
boots. At the landing I opened the door to my room. There
was a four poster bed with curtains looped back, a basin of
fresh water on the press and a cheerful fire crackling in the
narrow hearth. I closed the door with a sigh of mixed relief
and exhaustion. This would do nicely as a hideout until I had
word that my Night Wing was restored to me.

I was still rattled by the sight of Daniel. My mind turned from him to the twisting fear of a marauder going after my ship while she was beached in Stonehaven. There was a jug of madeira on the dresser. I quaffed two glasses then felt disgusted with myself. Wine and grog had been forced on me in those first months with Black Hal. I knew from experience it was no true escape from sorrow. I saw what it did to women, the fishwives and doxies who worked in the taverns and along the docks. Their lives, and whatever nice looks they had, were as good as thrown in a ditch. I remembered their veined cheeks and raucous tongues, how they lost any clear thought in their heads. If I had gone that way I would never have had the presence of mind to plot my way out of Hal's clutches.

I flung the empty glass across the room and watched it bounce against the bed post without shattering. It rolled across the floor, reminding me of the rock of the Night Wing's boards under my feet. Never again, I told myself, and not on account of a milksop who's complexion turns green at the thought of a good sea swell. I laughed at myself in the mirror glass then set to undressing from my wet clothes. After that I sponged myself in the basin of water, dried off and put on the warm wrap Lennox servant had left for me.

As I blew out the candles, I caught myself taking a surreptitious glance in the mirror. I knew I was comely, beautiful even, and not simply because frightened men liked to pay me compliments. Even after years at sea I had kept my fair complexion, covering myself in gloves and hats and shawls as protection from the weather as well as acting as disguise. My hair, when it wasn't coiled under a hat or pirate scarf, was thick, glossy and black as the raven that flew on the Night Wing's pennant. Mouth, full and red, eyes brown with a golden flash - eyes fit to drown in, one fine pirate had told me, and he knew his women if he knew anything.

Sometimes when I saw myself just woken from sleep, I was startled by a countenance so melting and open that men would believe they had a right to be in charge of me. That's why people didn't often see my face without mask or makeup. In the plain light of day I looked too fresh, too young. But as I looked at myself now, I found myself wondering if Daniel favoured black hair in women, or was moved by a ripe mouth.

I told myself this was folly brought on by the strain of worrying for my ship. I would think on it no more. Sliding between the cold sheets, my feet searched out the hot wrapped stone. I sent my mind to the Night Wing, not beached and maimed as I had last seen her. I remembered flying the blue ocean on my first voyage with her through Antillas Keys. We dropped anchor in water so clear you could swear you were looking down at the sky, not up. The crew swam and caught fresh turtle and flying fish. Trees swayed under bright stars, the air still balmy after the moon had full risen. I had slipped away to swim by myself in the ink dark sea around the bay. Afterwards I lay in the balmy breeze on the Night Wing's deck, lulled by the rippling waves. The memory of the warm Caribbean night and the soothing tilt of my ship dipped me into sleep.

CHAPTER 13

A bright morning woke me. Though the room was chill and my bed snug, I slipped out from under the covers. Opening the casement window I stuck out my head and listened to the sound of gulls keening overhead and the clatter of servants in the kitchen yard. Yesterday's rough voyage, clambering along the cliff path to the sanctuary of Lennox's house, seemed like a dream. As for Daniel Stede, I grimaced at the memory of my foolishness.

A brief scatter of rain wet my cheeks and the sun glanced out from behind the scudding clouds. I would pass the time till Catter arrived by reading in Lennox's fine library and taking long rides on one of his excellent horses. Flynn and the others could do what they would, Cameron and Gower would have time to recover from their injuries. As for our hostage, Lennox could see to his welfare. I would give Daniel no more thought until he was put in a boat back to his father and we were on our way to collect my mended Night Wing.

For six days the weather was fair and I lost myself in riding and long walks. Every night, Lennox did us proud at the dining table and those of the men who cared to would sit around the fire swapping tales till after midnight. At the end of the week I was beginning to fret about Catter's return but I joined the men as usual. There was an excellent rabbit pie followed by rich fruit cake and a new opened bottle of burgundy. Suddenly, I heard a shout from outside. Lennox stood up to investigate when a manservant opened the door.

"Boat spied in the bay."

"Does it give the signal?" Lennox said.

The servant nodded. "Two and three flashes of the lantern."

I clapped my hands and leapt to my feet. I ran the passage to the front door and stood in the porch, straining my eyes to watch for the boat landing. Lennox brought me a shawl then went to make arrangements for an extra bed to be set up. Flynn came out to join me, glass in hand, until we saw a lantern flare like a tiny spark at the foot of the cliff path. The wind was up, masking any sounds from the bay. After what seemed an age, a dark silhouette appeared at the top of the rise. In another few moments, Catter was before us, his great coat collar turned up against the cold and his boots spilling water from a clumsy leap ashore.

"No crew?" Flynn said.

"They set off directly on the tide turn." Catter's voice was thin with exhaustion.

I ran to him and grabbed him by the arm. "Devil take the crew. How goes it with Stede?"

I pulled him up the steps to the porch. In the lamplight his fine features sagged with tiredness. I sensed the other men gathering behind me in the hall.

"Catter?"

"He won't pay."

I stood as if struck.

"He won't pay and he won't parley. I've never known a man more stubborn."

"God's blood, does he not know we have his son?"

"I spelled it out, clear as I could, ma'am."

"You told him it was Queen Meg herself who has his precious boy, heir to his lands and fortune? His son is my prisoner, his very life is in the balance. Does he not understand?"

Catter grimaced. "Stede told me to tell Queen Meg he won't give in to pirate's blackmail. He offered threats, ma'am, said you'd better return the boy or he'll have a word in the King's ear and all the forces of the realm will be after you."

"I warned you."

This from Daniel who should have been hiding upstairs, not standing in the doorway, a challenge in his look.

"What in hell's name is he doing downstairs?"

"I thought you would want him to send back on the boat that brought Catter." Gower said. "You told us there would be a swift exchange with the ransom."

"There'll be no ransom," Daniel said.

"What if I send you back, piece by piece, a finger here, a bloody toe there? Doesn't your father care about you? Doesn't he want you to sire heirs for him, cosset his lands and his mansion?"

"He wants me to be strong, and cruel. What he considers a real man to be. That's why he sent me away to learn the harsh ways of the world, or so he told me."

I realised this was our first exchange since the kidnap more than ten days before. I was also struck by how unafraid Daniel seemed. He stared me down as though I were one of his servants. I faced him squarely and raised my voice.

"Is this not harsh enough for him? That you are under threat of death from pirate kidnappers."

Daniel spread his fine hands in a resigned gesture.

"We quarrelled often before I was sent away."

"It's a dire sort of tiff that would cause a man to abandon his only son."

"He fears I'll ruin my inheritance. The people who work on our estates have sorry lives." Daniel's face was suddenly animated, flushed. "I want to give them freehold property and help them set up with capital, so they can work the land proudly and sell and barter what they grow and tend, not have it taken off them with only a tithe given back. "

"You're a radical then." Lennox looked at Daniel with some contempt. "Your neighbouring lords would crush you before their own serfs started demanding cozy treatment too."

"Are we discussing politics or dealing with my prisoner and my missing ransom?"

Daniel cut across me as if I hadn't spoken. "Those landlords delude themselves if they think their serfs can be kept down forever."

I was speechless at his effrontery.

"Lennox is right," Flynn said. "Most landowners would think you're upsetting the ordained way of things."

"God in his heaven, the lord in his manor and his servants beneath all?" As he spoke, he looked directly at me. "Where do pirates fit into this great picture, Mistress Meg?"

"How dare you jibe at the pirate's life, something no landed gentry could ever understand. Gower, take him out of my sight."

Gower pinned Daniel's arms and bundled him upstairs. I looked around at the men.

"Stede will cough up that ransom if I have to hold a knife to his throat myself."

I loosed my dagger and flipped it expertly at the newel post. It lodged inches from Lennox's head. He blanched and recoiled a step backwards, almost knocking Stanmore down in the process. My little pantomime caused a laugh and achieved my intention of distracting the men from the outcome of my ransom plan. That it was a rank failure hit me square in the face, but I would not admit it openly.

"Catter, you look dead on your feet. Get some sleep and we'll review our plan in the morning."

Sending Catter off was my own excuse to retire before anyone detected how undone I was by the night's events. I bolted myself in my room and sank down in the bed. All my buoyant hope was run away like rain in a gutter. Now, I wondered how I could have been so stupid. My driving need to rescue the Night Wing had blinded me. I had counted on Stede's fear and weakness and now I was being taught a lesson.

On top of that, the scene with Daniel had shaken my nerve even further. I was entirely used to crewmen speaking only when they were told to. Daniel's confidence, his gentleman's speech, had lost me control of the situation. Lurking behind that was the dreadful fear that his father judged me with nothing but contempt, that he would never pay the ransom I depended on to save my ship, regardless of my threats.

CHAPTER 14

I tossed and turned until the sky lightened. My mind spun with half-formed plots against Stede, none of them useful. I kept picturing Daniel's face, vivid as he talked about social reform. He had reminded me of friends of my father, gathered in our sitting room, discussing politics in their educated accents. It was a life long lost to me.

I threw on a greatcoat and ran downstairs, startling a servant who was carrying coal to light the sitting room fire. There wasn't a horse ready saddled so I walked on to the coastal path, striding out as though my life depended on it. I barely noticed the landscape, sea to my right, rolling green hills to my left. After an hour my pace slackened. The early mist had lifted to reveal a sharp line of cliffs, edged with grass and grey shale. A thin track dropped to a narrow plateau a few feet below. Sunshine bounced around me, dazzling, as I scrambled down. My boots slipped on loose stones, and my fingers clutched at thick tufts of grass blown strong by the relentless sea breezes.

Once on the plateau, I leaned back against the cliff side, sheltered from the wind. I watched seagulls swoop and circle above the foaming waves then closed my eyes, squeezing them tight until all I could see was a daze of white. But she was still there, the girl I wanted to forget. Margaret Robinson, in a white dress, walked beside her father in the garden of a lovely mansion house. She had lived protected and innocent, in a world where bad things only happened in story books and every night was a prayer and a mother's hand on her hair.

Daniel. I knew it then, the breathless yearning he provoked in me was for much more than his handsome person. He was like a fresh-poured draught from my life before the kidnap. He reminded me of the time before my family was slaughtered and our home burned. Like Daniel, I had been educated, been refined like him. Then Hal had taken me when I was barely fourteen and Margaret Robinson had vanished in one night of black terror.

The pain in my heart felt as if it would wrench me in two. I couldn't bear it. Cursing Daniel for turning me into this moping thing, I scrambled back up to the path, berating myself as a fool for giving way to brooding. I knew full well what my life was about now. I had survived the worst, more than four years as Hal's puppet daughter.

I turned and stared out to the horizon. There was no sense in dwelling on what might have been. I couldn't change it, even by one day. I told myself it could have been worse. And if Hal had never come, perhaps I would be a dull, housebound lady, with no life beyond a husband and home. Why were my eyes running tears? I had learned much on Hal's foul ships. I could fight and command men, and had cultivated my sea-knowing to a legendary art. I was Queen Meg of the High Seas, untouchable. This grief that I would never be courted by a gentleman as fine as Daniel was a weak girl's humour. Besides, what was Daniel Stede except the means to get back my ship, and my freedom? As for desire, Queen Meg could take him for that too if she chose to.

The wind from the sea picked up and stung my damp cheeks. Watching the stream of darkening clouds, I realised I had lost track of time. I set my feet on the track again. I'd given myself a long walk back to Lennox's house and the wind blew against me the whole way. The waves foaming in the bay turned my thoughts back to the wounded Night Wing. My mind argued this way and that, whether to try another ransom threat for Stede or sail back to Stonehaven and seize my ship, with or without payment to Conroy for the repairs.

I was exhausted by the time I reached Lennox's house and let myself in the rear door. A serving girl emerged from the kitchen and I asked her to draw me a hot bath. I was on my way to Lennox's sitting room with the intention of borrowing a book when Lennox himself waylaid me in the hallway. He gave one curious look at my dishevelled appearance then stepped close to speak quietly.

"Mistress, there's something I heard this morning. It may be gossip but my source swears on it and I must tell you so you can be the judge."

I followed him into the sitting room. As usual, the fire was banked too warm for comfort. Lennox offered me a glass of brandy from the scatter of bottles on the black polished table. I waved the glass away.

"Good God Lennox, come the point of it, will you?"

Lennox poured himself a generous measure and gulped it down while I took the chair furthest from the hearth. The cushion behind my back was too thick for comfort and I discarded it on the floor. Lennox paced the room once then stood in front of me, passing his empty glass from one hand to the other.

"You won't like this. A man from Launceston, who I trust, sent word that Black Hal is sailing a fast ship to England, to Plymouth in fact. He's looking for you. Apparently, he caught wind of the boy's kidnap and put two and two together."

My skin crept with dread, but I didn't want Lennox to see my fear. "The last time I heard rumours of Hal's black hide was of him dying of the pox in New Guinea. Or was it marrying a Sultan's daughter in Tunis, or drowned off the Cape? You know he sends out most of the stories himself so why should this be any different?"

"Take heed. My friend's source met him in person and large as life in Marseilles. He bragged he'd all but sunk the Night Wing."

I looked at him soberly. "Flynn heard the rumour, too. But I think I shall go mad if I believe it. Besides, where on God's earth would he get coin or friends to beg or steal such a vessel?"

"It seems there's a tale of him ransoming a Sultan's daughter."

I burst out laughing. The notion was too outrageous, even for Hal.

"Did he charm her with his wit or his scrawny belly? Or was it his skill in abducting children that won her over?"

Lennox didn't join in my laughter. "In a manner of speaking, it was," he said. "The girl had been kidnapped by the

Sultan's cousin. He would have put her to death if Hal hadn't snatched her. It was a case of being in the right place at the right time and seizing an opportunity. The upshot was a daughter restored and a treasure chest for Hal. He bought a ship and spent half the gold on fitting it out. He named the ship Hell's Mouth. It flies a pure black sail."

I leapt from my seat and stood still, my back to Lennox, the blood chilling in my veins. So it was a fact, the ship that had ambushed us, broken the Night Wing, belonged to Hal.

"His boast was that the Night Wing will be his one day." Lennox mouth set in an uncharacteristic grim line. "And, to quote the words my source remembered, so will 'my fair Meg, my own daughter Queen' or so Hal calls you."

I gripped my hands together. My expression was under control but I was shocked to hear the terror in my voice. "What would he find out in Plymouth? He'll never trace us here."

"In time, with enough careful bribes and patient threats, he could. And if you're bent on sending more envoys to Lord Stede, you could set a trail for Hal to follow. Besides, it doesn't look as though any ransom is forthcoming."

"That's all bluster on Stede's part. He'll come round soon enough when he realises we're not giving up his son easily. Lennox, how soon can you find us a seaworthy barque?"

"Where are you planning to go?"

"Gibraltar, or maybe Malta or Spanish Morocco. If this story about Black Hal is true then we'll skip south and under his reach until he loses the scent or until we can fetch the mended Night Wing, whichever comes first."

"It's too dangerous. You'll be seen in this port or that and word will get back to him, especially if he's bent on it. Crossing the Channel once was enough of a risk."

"Then what do you advise? Sit here till Hal takes us from our beds and burns your house into the bargain?" Gratefully, I felt my terror give way to anger. "Well? What are you waiting for?"

Lennox shook his head then threw up his hands in resignation. "Give me a few hours. I can't be seen to be desperate. We don't want anyone asking more questions than necessary."

"There must be a sloop or barque somewhere. I suppose the one we came in is long gone?"

Lennox nodded. "It's no loss. Besides, you'll need better than that to cross to Morocco or beyond. And a bigger crew."

He gave me a last warning look as he hurried out the door to find his horse. I stood for a long moment, making sure I had control of my chaotic emotions. I was bursting to raise the house and have us packed within the hour. Instead, I walked upstairs to make the best of my tepid bath water.

I soaped and rinsed, trying to calm myself. Lennox must have told Flynn on his way out because the Quartermaster was soon knocking at my door. Childishly, I didn't want to speak to him. I would have to admit that Hal had us on the run. When I didn't answer, Flynn knocked louder and added a few kicks for good measure. I leapt out of the bath, wrapped a blanket around myself and flung the door open. Flynn looked as angry and worried as I felt.

"This is foolhardy, ma'am. I beg you, we should go inland, lose ourselves in the countryside, not make ourselves easy pickings out at sea."

"Said your piece?"

"No, mistress. You know I'd go to the ends of the world and back in your service."

"Then why are you not getting the men ready to leave?"

"Because it looks as though we're running willy-nilly in fear of Black Hal."

It stung that Flynn could see the depth of my panic.

"Go where you like and the devil take you, but I'm hiring a boat and sailing south."

"We'll need extra hands for such a journey. More men is more risk of loose tongues."

"Lennox is seeing to it."

"You've got that man under a spell that will see him killed one day."

"Lennox can take care of himself." I went to close the door in Flynn's face. He stayed it with a hand. I scowled at him. Flynn was always loyal and, often as not, right in his judgement, but today I couldn't afford to listen to him. "Make ready, Quartermaster. Like it or not, we sail." I slammed the door and threw the bolt.

CHAPTER 15

I had my way. How else could it be? But, after we paid the rest of my ready gold for the sloop Lennox found us, the money was still short. The thieving Breton whose boat it was followed Lennox back to the house and walked in with half a dozen of his thugs. His jaw dropped when he saw me standing in the hallway. Behind me, my men and Daniel were assembled and ready to leave.

"You're her. Queen Meg, as I live and breathe."

"I'm a phantom. You never saw me."

The Breton squared his shoulders.

"I'm here for the rest of my money."

I glanced at Lennox.

"Did he honour his side of the bargain?"

Lennox nodded. "Boat's docked and ready in the bay."

In one stride I grabbed Daniel's hand, wrenched the ring from it and tossed it to the Breton. I noticed Daniel didn't even try to resist.

"That's to settle." I spat on my gloved hand and held it out. The man took it, reluctantly. His eyes never left my face. I stared him down. "I can see what you're thinking. Your mind is figuring that my person would fetch a ransom ten times the price of your boat."

He flushed. "A man can't help his thoughts."

In a flash my naked cutlass was at his throat. "Then be sure to keep them to yourself and no harm done."

Joshua and Flynn drew their own swords as I pushed the Breton away. He ran, his men behind him. Joshua frowned.

"Should have silenced him, ma'am. Shall we go after them?"

"We'll be out to sea by the time he reaches the village." I smiled, to cover that I knew Joshua was right. Haste and fear were making me careless. I should have kept my face hidden. Once seen, why didn't I make a clean kill of it, stopped the Breton's wagging tongue? Or at the least, have him and his men locked up till we were well away.

Catter, Joshua and Gower clattered up the wide staircase to bring our packed boxes. They stacked them by the door, ready for the wagon. Pedlar, shifting uneasily on his bandaged leg, tied Daniel's wrists. Daniel pulled against him, protesting.

"Is this to be my life? Being dragged from one place to another on these pointless escapades?"

"Your life is what we tell you it is."

Daniel yanked at the rope, pulling it from Pedlar's grip. Like a fool, he tried to make a run for it but Joshua had him before he took two paces. He fought though, I'll give him that. It took both Joshua and Gower to grapple him to his knees. He buckled over with a wail of despair and frustration. Tears streamed down his cheeks.

"My father will never pay ransom, I'm telling you!"

"He'll pay! He'll pay or we'll slit your throat. In the meantime you'll do as you're told."

"Let me go. I swear I'll ask my father to loan me the money for your ship."

"You think we'd let you loose to run home?"

"At least I have a home to run to. What sort of life do you have, hiding from everyone, a price on your head?"

I was taken aback. He spoke as though he pitied me rather than feared for his own life. There was an uncomfortable pause then Gower dragged him to his feet and hustled him to the door. I went to follow but Lennox took me by the arm and pulled me aside. He spoke quietly in my ear.

"Leave the young lord with me. I'll hide him and send another ransom note on your behalf. He's useless cargo otherwise."

"We'll drop him at the next port. You've done enough for us already."

Lennox shifted closer. "I can dispose of him easy enough."

I heard the scuffle as they dragged Daniel outside. I didn't turn around. Lennox gave me a knowing look. I met his gaze. He had seen right through me. The sad fact was I couldn't let Daniel go, not yet. I shook Lennox's hand, sharply grateful for his loyalty. Lennox kissed me on each cheek then stood back.

Suddenly, through the open door, I caught the wild, wet scent of the ocean. The sea was all around us yet it seemed as though it had been a bare whisper with my mind so full of phantoms and uncertainties. I ran outside to follow the others to the waiting barque.

Within the hour we were away, the rolling tide under us. Thoughts of Hal sneaking across the Channel had scrambled any premonitions that might have come to me but as soon as my feet touched sea timber it was as though the clouds lifted from my mind.

"Flynn, have them change the rigging, we go west."

"Not south along the coast? "

"I can feel it – there's a strong wind brewing, a day's hence." It was true, the prickling in my skin, dulled on land, was sharp as a whistle. There would be rough winds and heavy swells. "We sail west, then north to Cornwall."

"Black Hal could still be in Plymouth."

Suddenly, I felt sure about him too.

"Not him. He wouldn't risk being sold out. There's a high price on his head in Plymouth port. Too many people know him and he made dire enemies of more than a few. He'll run back to Spain." I stood close to Flynn so the Breton crew couldn't hear me. "This is the plan, Master Flynn. We'll dock on the Cornish coast and pay a messenger to take the next ransom note. After that we'll sail back through the Channel, ahead of the storm, and make our way north to Scotland and the Night Wing."

I stood astride to balance against the tilt of the barque. I imagined being reunited with my dear mended ship, and I thought of Daniel, stowed safe below.

CHAPTER 16

We sailed at speed for two days. As I predicted, the storm was black on the horizon behind us. My confidence grew with every smooth mile while the last threads of storm clouds drifted away like smoke. Yet I couldn't stop my thoughts straying towards Daniel. It was like an obsession. On the third day I found myself pacing the deck timbers for an hour or more. My impulse got the better of me. I ran below and, with a brief knock, threw open the door to Gower's cabin. Daniel sat on the upper bunk, eating a plate of something from the cook's pot. Gower leapt to his feet when I appeared in the doorway. The cabin was untidy with bedclothes strewn about and last night's supper dishes on the small table.

"Ma'am."

"Is our prisoner behaving himself?"

"He's not so sick as last time, if that's what you mean, ma'am."

"Is that right, Daniel?"

Daniel nodded politely, his face impassive. "The voyage seems smoother."

He looked pale in spite of finding his appetite. I felt a stab of remorse at having him cooped up in Gower's sour smelling cabin.

"Perhaps you're finding your sea legs. Come with me and help pen another letter to your father."

Gower raised his eyebrows but said nothing as he untied the rope that secured Daniel's wrists to the bed frame.

"Call if you need, ma'am."

I patted my cutlass and dagger and gave him a wink.

"I believe I'll be quite safe, Master Gower."

Crouching under the low timbers, I led the way to my tiny cabin. Out of the fresh air, the boat stank of mildew. There had been no time to fumigate or stack bunches of dried lavender and pine as we did on the Night Wing.

"How do you like the pirate's life so far?" My heart beat fast, as though I was readying for a skirmish.

Daniel didn't reply. As I closed the door behind us I found he was standing too close in the confined space. I lit the single lamp and the warm glow of it etched his fine profile. We were silent, regarding each other. Above us were muffled noises from the men on deck and the creak and heave of the barque as we swung on the even waves. I could see the beat of a pulse in Daniel's neck, a glisten of sweat on his upper lip.

"Have you always been – this?" He gestured, his two hands tied together, taking in the boat, my wide brimmed hat, cutlass and boots, me.

His question broke the spell. I snapped open the lid of my sea chest and drew out a leather wallet of paper, ink and quills. I pointed to the single chair.

"Sit down and write."

He hesitated then slumped down on and held out his hands for me to untie them. I snapped the rope with my dagger.

There was a pause as I pointed the blade at his throat. Our eyes met.

"What shall I write?"

"'My dear father' of course."

"He would know these aren't my words. I would address him as 'Sir.'"

"Sir, then."

I tucked the dagger in my belt and watched him write, watched his hands. He had never mentioned the ring I'd plucked from them. I adopted a mock serious tone as I dictated the letter.

"I entreat you to consider my captors' most generous terms. As yet I have not been harmed and I keep in good health. But I beg you not to stretch their tolerance further. They will dispose of me most cruelly if you refuse to send half the ransom by return messenger, the other half to be paid when I am brought safe to you. Your dear obedient son, la-de-dah and so forth."

Daniel wrote, signed his name and put down the quill. His eyes met mine. He looked angry.

"This will never work. And what then?"

"I'll tell him if he doesn't send the gold I want by the next full moon, I'll marry you. The sons of a pirate wench will inherit his lands when he's dead. How would he like that, Master Daniel?"

He flushed and looked away. I studied his pale neck, the line of his jaw.

"And how would you like it?" I said. Somewhere above I heard the rumble of casks being rolled as the men tidied the decks. "Or are you betrothed already?"

"My father wishes me to marry a cousin."

"Ah – the daughter of the aunt who lives in Looe. Do you wish it?"

"No. I wish – "

Suddenly, I glimpsed his wish. Too young, I had learned to know when a man wanted me. It was my instinct and survival and I couldn't fault it. The skin prickled on my neck. I was the very opposite of a genteel lady yet Daniel was in my hands. I was shaken by desire and a sharp sense of victory.

Two long minutes passed. At the end of them followed a sobering thought. Daniel wanted me in spite of himself and he would come to loathe me for it. I reached for the letter, brushed his hand, saw his fingers tremble. I felt his eyes on me as I turned my back and opened the silver writing case. Taking out wax and ribbon, I sealed the folded parchment and stamped it with my ring, the emblem of a hawk, pressed into the soft red.

I imagined Daniel reaching out his hand, pulling me to him. I knew he would not resist me should I try him. With an effort in every step, I left the cabin, not caring that Daniel was unguarded. I looked around for someone to escort him back to Gower's cabin. It was Flynn who I ran into. If he noticed anything amiss he didn't remark on it.

"Take the prisoner back to Gower. I brought him to my cabin for a moment. He penned a ransom note that I hope will do the trick." I held up the sealed letter.

"Stede's in your cabin?"

There was a long pause. I stared Flynn down, daring him to pass comment about Daniel. After a moment, I stepped past him.

"I'll be on deck. It should be a clear night. We'll reach landfall by midmorning."

"The worst time to go ashore, in full view of curious eyes."

"We'll make safe anchor a good way off. I'm sending Joshua with the ransom note. He can row a boat in himself. No one else needs to step foot ashore. Joshua can find a horse and take the letter directly to Stede. We'll have a few days to ply the coast until he returns. We may even come across some booty."

I leaned forward and slapped him on the shoulder. Flynn was having none of my false gaiety. His expression, shadowed in the cramped and ill-lit galley, looked grim.

"I know this bit of the coast. It's all poor villages and fishing boats."

"And smugglers' coves. You recall what Dead Man Jones told us the last time we were in Falmouth? There are three or four caves where the smugglers think their treasure safe for months. This is the perfect time and opportunity to explore them."

My cabin door swung open and Daniel appeared, stooping his head under the low ceiling. Flynn turned at the sound and I hurried above decks. I needed time to think about what to do with Daniel, or rather what I should do, while I was still capable of good judgement.

CHAPTER 17

The morning broke with dull weather, a light drizzle of rain and a sea mist in our favour. We cruised along the coast as the sun slowly dispersed the fog. I felt strangely agitated, from excitement or a warning, I couldn't tell. I thought my sleep would be riddled with thoughts of Daniel but I had rested well. It was as if confirming the attraction between us had settled something in me, for the time being at least.

We dropped anchor well off the coast. Joshua was already dressed and packed with a bag of provisions. I handed him the sealed letter that Daniel had penned.
"Ready to be my emissary to Lord Stede?"
"Honoured, m'lady."
"The ransom note is from his son's own hand. Stede is bound to take notice this time. As soon as you have his reply and, God willing, half the ransom money, make haste back to us. We'll ply the coast then hide up country near Falway and keep lookout for you there. I estimate three days at the most for you to travel to Stede's estate, do your business and rejoin us. We'll wait inland near Redbridge and look out for you."
"I'll bring your gold myself."
I patted his shoulder.
"I hope it doesn't go too hard with you, a poacher having to parlay with m'lord."
His face broadened into a wide grin, showing his one gold tooth. "It goes very well indeed."
I watched as he climbed down to the row boat and set off to shore. An hour later we pulled anchor and set sail again. I remembered Dead Man Jones hinting that the smugglers' cache lay north of Torsand harbour, so there we travelled. It was late in the morning when we dropped two boats in the water. In one boat were Flynn and four men. In the other

boat with me were Gower, Pedlar, much recovered from his leg wound, one of the French crew, Stanmore and Daniel. Gower frowned when he saw Daniel climbing down to join us.

"Shouldn't you leave him on board ship?"

"I don't trust our Breton captain. He has an inkling Daniel may be worth something and could decide to take him as his own prisoner."

It was partly true. The other part was that I wanted Daniel to see me in my element, a true adventuring pirate. If I couldn't be a fine lady, still I might change his view from scorn to admiration.

As soon as we set off in the boats, we could smell smoke. My heart beat fast as we scanned the coast, trying to see where fires had been lit. The frisson of adventure gave way to vague dread. Scattered shouts, echoing from the next bay, intensified my fear. We rowed on in silence. There was a stray gunshot. As we rounded the bay of Torsand, smoke billowed thick towards us.

From the head of the reef we could see fisherman's houses, picked out in their blue and whitewashed colours, tumbled down to the harbour. But that gay sight was eclipsed by a black-sailed ship anchored in the bay. Along the shore, cottages, boats and barns blazed fire. The screams of women and children rent the air as a band of pirates dragged them from their homes. Standing at the prow of the bobbing ship, large as life, was Black Hal.

Gower and Flynn were already trying to turn the row boats to get out of sight and range. The chill of dread suddenly exploded to red rage inside me.

"Flynn!" I yelled at the other boat. "Follow me! I'll stop this black devil once and for all. Row!" I ordered Gower in my own boat. "Bring us alongside so he can see who he's dealing with."

"Mistress!" Gower's mouth was agape with fear. "Come away. There's no hope of taking them. I count twenty of the blackguards at least."

I threw myself on the oars, berating the men until they were forced to comply. Even Daniel did as I bid. We rapidly closed the distance between us and the black ship. One of Hal's pirates saw us and yelled a warning. Black Hal turned, raced to the ship's side and whooped with glee. His voice carried thin across the distance.

"Meg! My own girl! Look at the booty." He gestured to the boxes and furniture that were being dragged from the houses. "Come share it with me. You're my own Queen Meg, ain't you?"

He laughed, a cackle I knew all too well when he was drunk, not with ale but the thrill of a massacre. God knows I had led enough raids myself, but not in this bloodthirsty, wanton spree that Hal loved so much. I was determined to stop him. I turned to Gower.

"Take us to shore." Gower's face set grimly as he gestured Daniel and the others to turn the boat landward. "Row, damn you." The men bent harder to the oars. I saw the Frenchman glance at me with fear. Within moments we were sliding into the shallows of Torsand Bay, where Hal's men were throwing booty into their own row boats. Our manoeuvre took them by surprise and they lost moments before they realised what I was about.

I leapt from our boat and waded ashore, rapier and cutlass unsheathed, cutting Hal's men down as I went. Handicapped as they were with their arms full of spoils, I finished four of them before they could defend themselves. Blazing with anger, I swung around to face Hal himself where he stood at the prow of Hell's Mouth. My skirts were awash with bloody water.

"Come down here in a fair fight!"

Hal laughed and pulled a jeering face, seemingly undaunted by the sight of his men cut down in front of his eyes.

"No – you come to me, Meg! Here, where you belong."

Flynn yelled a warning. The rest of Hal's pirates were racing along the beach, abandoning their spoils to come after us.

Turning, I ran towards them, still in a fever of blood lust and rage. A billow of smoke blew across the beach, distorting the villagers' screams and the sound of musket shot coming from the Hell's Mouth. Through the mist I saw a girl, barely a teenager, her dress torn, hair matted with blood, mouth open in a silent scream.

"You black bastards!" I felt my arms suddenly pinned as I was almost brought to my knees by Gower. Pedlar joined him to stop me before I could run up the shore to rescue the girl. Between them they dragged me back to our boat, threw me inside and began rowing for their lives while I railed at them for every sort of coward.

"Do you know what he'll do to her? Murder her family and worse!"

The Frenchman yelled in my face. "Asseyez-vous!" He tried to push me down in the boat. "What sort of hell-cat are you?"

I lunged at him, went to strike him across the face, and fell short as the boat caught speed and darted out into the bay.

Daniel's voice cut through the din. "If you stay to be killed you can't help anyone." His face was set but calm. The boat pitched and I landed hard in my seat, my eyes locked on his. Something about Daniel's steady gaze broke through my madness. Suddenly, I was myself again. I seized an oar and pulled along with the others.

Gower rowed desperately, turning his head to look back in the bay. "He'll come after us."

"Yes, but we have a brief space while they load their spoils and whatever villagers they haven't killed." My mind was cool again, my instincts clear. "The mist is drifting south, it should hide us while we race him to the next bay."

We were close to the edge of the sandy cliff that marked Torsand's edge. As we bent hard to the oars, the sound of musket fire and screams receded. I took a last glance behind us as we turned out of the bay. Through the mist I could make out the sails of Hal's ship. As I predicted, it was still at anchor.

CHAPTER 18

The current was with us as we raced towards the waiting sloop. Hal would expect me to bring reinforcements for an all-out battle. Sadly, our hired Breton ship was ill-equipped for a sea skirmish. But the thought hatched a plan in my my mind. I was first off the row boat to climb the rope snaking up the ship's side. The captain grabbed my hand to help me on deck then took a step back when he saw my bloodied skirts.

"Who attacked you?"

"We have Black Hal himself at our backs. I'll pay you over the odds for this old bucket of a sloop if you get everyone on shore and abandon ship."

The captain shook his head, frowning. "He'll catch us on land as surely as on board."

"If you're willing to part with it, I plan to booby trap your ship with explosives." I pointed to the lip of the bay. "When Hal's finished looting, it's certain he'll come looking for me. With luck, he'll open fire and be blown to kingdom come."

I turned to look at Gower and Flynn as they jumped on board. Their expressions told me they had heard my plan.

Flynn was the first to speak. "What if Hal doesn't take the bait?"

Suddenly, the air felt sharp as ice, the blue sky pulsed with light. I heard my voice, as clear as a bell chiming across the water.

"He'll be lured south and into the path of the storm, a storm blowing quick and sudden before evening."

The captain crossed himself. He had heard of my preternatural sense of wind and weather. We fixed on a price for his boat and he gave the order to raise anchor. We rode the current to the long stretch of sand known as Heron's Bay and moored in as close as we could. Mist drifted down from the cliff tops as everyone ferried to shore with our goods and chattels. Meanwhile, Catter stayed on board, directing a couple of reluctant Bretons to lace the decks with as much gunpowder and pitch as they could find.

I paced the beach, eyes stretched for any sight of a black sail. Catter made quick work of the sloop and he and the French crew, disembarked, cut the anchor line and rowed safely to shore. We watched silently as the ship bobbed and turned with the tide. For a chilling moment I thought we had stayed too late then she caught the wind, bucked lightly into the current and set sail in the direction of Torsand. If Hal came looking for us, he'd sail straight at the sloop.

We struggled uphill from the shore. Most of the crew had already scattered, carrying what they could of their belongings. At Flynn's urging I set off with my own men and the Breton who was staying close with a few of his men to ensure payment for his ship. I had no gold. There would be a bitter fight with the Bretons. I would have to give surety above the odds, but it would be worth it if my plan succeeded. As we crested the rise, I took a last glance back at the unmanned sloop. I imagined Hal's jeering face when the sloop suddenly loomed out of the mist and he hit a broadside at it. I fervently hoped that this time it would be the end of him. My mind was still haunted by the sight and screams of the girl from the village, fleeing in terror from fire and Hal's men.

We were a couple of miles into the moors when Flynn fell into pace alongside me.

"A word, mistress."

His face gave little away except for a glint of suppressed excitement I recognised from the more successful of our adventures. Taking his cue, I walked more briskly until we were a few yards ahead of the others and out of earshot. Flynn reached inside his tunic and drew out a sodden cloth bag. When he put it in my hand I felt the unmistakable weight and bulge of coin. I drew the string and stared at the handfuls of gold and silver inside. My jaw dropped open.

Flynn tapped his nose knowingly. "A gift from the village bailiff, courtesy of Black Hal's thieves. It was a lucky stroke they had dumped their booty at the shore by the time we were on land. They were too busy being cut through by Queen Meg to notice me helping myself."

"Flynn, you've saved our necks on many an occasion, but you outdid yourself this time! I thought I would have to slit the Breton's throat before he realised I had nothing to pay him for his sloop. There's more than enough here. Thank God." I clutched the bag to my chest then quickly hid it inside my coat.

"More than enough, mistress." Flynn's grin spread wider. "There's another like it still tucked in my bag." He flicked the bag's strap with his thumb. I burst out laughing and clapped him on the shoulder. "Oh Flynn, what a pirate you are! Take a handful of coin for yourself, as much as you care to. We'll pay off the Breton and have food in our bellies tonight and horses by tomorrow."

Flynn grinned again, his chest swelling with pride. I turned to the others and waited for them to catch up. Behind me, Flynn set his bag down and drew out another bag of coins. He weighed it in his hand, took out some gold and tied the drawstring again. Walking over to be Breton captain, he clapped the bag in his hand. The Breton looked at me.

"That should cover you for a new vessel," I said. "Any of you sailors that want to come north with us, you're welcome. The rest of you will be paid, as long as you take an oath of secrecy, in blood."

In the end, eight of the men came with us, the rest took their money and took an oath. Meanwhile, the captain made a long job of counting the gold, complaining all the while in guttural French. But it was obvious there was enough coin to buy him a better vessel than the old bucket we had just destroyed. I was still dazed at the turn of luck Flynn had brought us.

We stayed at Falway that night, not in the warm beds we'd promised ourselves but in a barn on land owned by an old crony of Lennox. Stanmore and Catter did us proud. By first light they had fetched food supplies and found a man willing to trade a couple of wagons and enough horses to give us a good start on our journey north. They had brought a couple of the horses with them in advance of the rest. Itching to set off north, I opened the barn door on the men who were still sleeping.

"It's a cold morning but a bright one. You can all take a dip in the river. I don't want you stinking to high heaven even before we start our ride."

Most of them crawled out of their makeshift beds and did as I bid. Those that refused were plunged in the river anyway. We made a good breakfast of bread, farm cheese and milk and sorted our bags and supplies while the rest of the horses were fetched.

Though Gower still kept a close eye on him, Daniel was left unbound to mingle with the men. Since he'd been involved in our escape from the black ship, a change had happened. It wasn't that he could be counted as one of us, and God knows what he thought of me now, murderess and lunatic most like, but he had kept his nerve in acute danger. Even Flynn noted that, since his outburst at Lennox's house, we had never heard a word of complaint from Daniel Stede.

It was still early morning when we set off. Pedlar and Cameron rode ahead as scouts. It was in the mid afternoon when Pedlar galloped back over the rise to join us. Breathless, he reined his horse.
"There's an inn at the next crossroads. The landlord was talking of rumours that a ship was blown up near the coast."

I sucked in a breath. "What else?"

"Not good, ma'am. They say the wrackers found little to salvage.from it. As to any other ship destroyed, either no one knows or no one's telling."

A black gloom settled on me as it looked more than likely Black Hal had escaped and I'd tindered a good ship for nothing.

CHAPTER 19

Two nights later we were billeted in miserable lodgings in a farmer's leaky outhouse, close to Redbridge where we had arranged to meet Joshua. Flynn was making preparations for our long ride north at a ruined barn half a mile off. He was unsure of some of the new crew members and had enlisted a couple more men who were seeking fortune beyond their village.

It was full moonrise when Cameron found Joshua and escorted him directly to me. I could tell on both their faces that the ransom had failed. It seemed that, apart from Flynn's miraculously salvaging the bags of coin, our luck slid from bad to worse.

Reluctantly, I walked with Joshua down the hill to break the bad news to Flynn. Drawing near, I could see the outline of ruined buildings, lantern light and the flickering shadows of men. Flynn hurried towards us, out of earshot of the new recruits. He saw all by my face and Joshua's dejected posture.

"Stede has refused us, even on his son's life."

"He all but laughed in my face before he threw me off the doorstep."

"How can he hold out so long?" Flynn spat on the dark grass. "He should know how lucky he is. Any other pirate would have sent his son back in a barrel."

"And it's not as if he can't afford it," Joshua said. I could see he' d taken his failure badly. "He has a very fine and fancy house and lands and plenty of men to do his bidding. He threatened to set four of them on me if I didn't 'ride back to hell' - those were his words. I believe he plans to bring the law down on you, ma'am."

"He has to catch me first."

I wiped the moist sea tang off my lips then realised I was crying, grizzling tears like a weak girl. I pulled my wide brimmed hat further down to cover my face, gripped the hilt of my cutlass and strode back up the hill. Taking a deep, stuttering breath, I made myself think about the Night Wing.

At this moment she was being mended, rigged and ready in the harbour. I had a crew fresh for the ocean and all that stood in my way was a pile of gold.

In another stride it was as clear as tide turning. There was nothing in my way if I chose it so. I would give Conroy the coin that Flynn had salvaged, though it was a bare quarter of the money I owed him. I had my main store of gold in a treasure chest in the Antilles - I just had to get to it. It was a bad thought that I would have to cheat Conroy in the meantime. But, putting that aside, I had in my grasp one ship and one ready crew. And the sum of that meant I could take to sea, free and flying, once again a match for Black Hal or any buccaneer.

I slept little that night, mostly plagued by conscience about cheating on my deal with Conroy. It was a low sort of pirate who dishonoured a promise. Even the murderers and thieves were superstitious about breaking the pirate's code. I had never done such a thing myself and hated to see in my men's faces what they would think of it, especially Flynn. The next morning I rose early and set off to tell him my plan, determined to brazen it out. As usual, he was up before anyone else, standing alone by a makeshift campfire, nursing a steaming cup.

"Flynn, do you have a fine crew for me?"

"Good enough, milady."

"Are they primed and ready for a quick act of piracy?"

"I'd say most of them are ready for little else. But what plan is there without the ransom money?"

"The plan is to ride north as fast as maybe then send a half dozen men to drag Master Conroy from his bed."

Flynn looked horrified.

"Don't pull such a face, Quartermaster. The Night Wing is surely mended by now, the Night Wing is mine and I intend to board and sail her the very hour we reach Stonehaven."

"You mean to steal her."

"I'm taking what's mine. Conroy will understand when I explain he'll have his payment in a couple of months or so. And now I'm going to breakfast and get ready to ride. I suggest you rouse the men to do the same. We have some days of hard travel ahead of us."

Our journey north met with clear weather though everyone was sunk in a black mood, especially Flynn. There were still problems with the new recruits and a shortage of horses. In the end, we retained about half, being those we could afford horses for, and let go the rest. On top of his wasted efforts in that quarter, I could see Flynn was angry at my cheating Conroy. I hated to think of it myself but I couldn't face the prison of being landlocked any more. After the botched encounter with Hal, and the sting of being bested by Stede, nothing was going to keep me from getting back on board the Night Wing.

Stonehaven was as damp and bleak as I remembered. Flynn and I left the men and horses on the outskirts of the town and went directly to the Red Star where Cal had a room. It was three in the morning but we roused him anyway. Never mind that the ransom scheme had failed and I had been tricked by Harry into the bargain, when Cal met us, dishevelled from sleep but with a smile on his lips, I felt my heart lift.

"Your ship is seaworthy," Cal said. "The shipwright worked his men like demons and has come up as good as his word."

I wished my own end of the bargain still held, but it couldn't be helped. Nothing else mattered but that I would stand on the Night Wing's deck again.

"You've seen her with your own eyes?"

"Seen and touched her, ma'am. The broken timbers are replaced, stronger than before, and all masts and rigging checked."

I let out a sigh.

"Then we set sail right away."

Cal frowned. "The shipwright is still abed. And the ship is guarded by four of his men."

I could not afford to hesitate. I heard my voice hard and cold. "Bring Conroy to the hill above the harbour and send another contingent to dispose of the guards. I want the Night Wing released to me right away."

"At night and by force?" I heard the accusation in Flynn's voice, saw Cal's bewilderment.

"Do my bidding, gentlemen. You have plenty of men for the job, Mr Flynn."

Flynn gave a helpless gesture then turned on his heel. Cal hurried after him, his face still a picture of confusion.

The half hour I walked up and down that wind-blown and moonlit ridge felt like the longest wait of my life. They brought Conroy at last, a blanket wrapped around his nightshirt. I could hear his cursing and railing all the way up the hill. I wished he didn't resist so hard, it made my actions seem even worse.

"Mr Conroy."

I stepped towards them, Flynn and Cal and three others surrounding Conroy who struggled in the midst of them. His grey hair was loose from the ribbon but in spite of his dishevelled appearance he still carried his dignity. I felt my betrayal of him keenly but the man stood between me and my immediate freedom.

"Mr Conroy, I have a deal for you."

He glared at me.

"I need my ship, you see."

I paced up and down in front of him. He stared at me wordlessly.

"You understand that, don't you?"

"I understand I was stupid to believe I could trust a pirate, for all your handshakes and talk of pirate's honour."

"Ah, there you are mistaken. You will have your gold and more, a tithe more, Mister Conroy, for your forbearance. I have money stored overseas."

"Why should I believe you?"

"Because you have no choice."

"How dare you threaten me!" At my gesture one of the men clapped a hand to Conroy's mouth to silence him. The shipwright struggled like the very devil.

"I'm sorry that your mood leaves no doubt you'll call the militia on us," I said, over his muffled protests. "We'll lock you up for a couple of days until we are sailed well clear. There'll be food and water, and blankets. I'll send a messenger to your family in Stirling. By the time they come for you, we'll be a memory on the horizon."

Conroy wrenched free of his captor's hand. "You evil, conniving bitch."

"Don't make things worse, Mister Conroy. I thank you for your work on my ship and I pledge you'll see the debt paid in due course. Good day to you."

I turned on my heel, filled with disgust at myself. The truth was, our Master Shipwright had shamed me, and more than a little.

CHAPTER 20

Cal had spoken truly. The Night Wing was mended strongly, beautifully. Her masts stood straight as the finest tree. I felt her restored, her even balance as soon as we floated her in the harbour less than an hour later. I had also felt, on the wind and by the moon, that the current was perfect for our sailing. Stifling my guilt, I reasoned that it was imperative to sail right then and there, regardless of the business with

Conroy. It would have been foolhardy to miss such a perfect tide turning.

I had been itching to sail for so long that even when we were two days at sea and my fine boat bucked nicely beneath me, I still prowled the deck like a mewling cat. The horizon ran a curve of blue against the flat sky and the ocean spread endlessly around us. I leaned on the windlass and stared out across the empty miles. I couldn't shake off the picture of Conroy's face when we locked the door of his temporary prison on him. His expression was more contempt than anger. I paced the deck again then saw Stanmore appear on deck. He had been put in charge of Daniel. I saw a chance of distracting my uneasy thoughts.

"Is Daniel settled?"

"Fighting the sea sickness again."

"Bring him up, then. Fresh air should help."

I did another round of the deck while Daniel was brought. Stanmore tethered him to a capstan where he could catch the breeze amidships. I walked casually to stand at the ship's rail, a couple of feet away from him.

"Watch the horizon," I said. "I'm told that when your eyes see a steady horizon, your stomach eases."

He looked startled to see me, then without a word did as I bid him. I kept him in my sidelong glance and after a while I saw him heave a breath and settle more comfortably on his seat. I shifted to stand closer to him. This was taking my mind off Conroy nicely.

I stroked the newly polished timber of the ship's rail. "She's beautiful, isn't she?"

Daniel's eyes flashed an unguarded look at mine and there it was once more, in spite of himself - desire.

"The Night Wing is the finest ship on the ocean."

"I couldn't say," Daniel said.

"We'll have a grand voyage."

"It wasn't a fine start though, was it?"

I stared at his profile as he looked back out to sea.

"Are you judging me, Master Stede?"

I stepped my boot sharply on the rope that tethered him, causing him to jerk sideways. He glared at me.

"I heard you cheated an honest man," he said.

I could feel the breath hot in my nostrils. So the crew had been talking about Conroy. I wanted to strike Daniel's handsome face.

"But that is the nature of pirates, I suppose," he said.

He stood up and leaned over the side as far as the tether rope allowed. For my part I turned away to pace the deck, to get away from him and his insolence. The mainsail caught a gust, billowed white against the blue sky. My beautiful ship, how could Daniel not understand? Without the Night Wing I was landlocked, dead. The wind scurried past and the sail dropped. A thread of odour from the Seat of Ease caught in my throat.

I gestured to Cal as he walked by. "This deck is filthy. Make sure it's swabbed before nightfall. And clean that foul latrine."

I rounded the deck and went below, slamming my cabin door. I hid myself away for the afternoon, angry, most of all with myself, for displaying such a fit of pique, like a spoiled child. My mood soured as the hours slid by. I felt humiliated that the men had gossiped about my treatment of Conroy, frustrated that I could hardly punish them for it. In the end I stayed below until we put in for supplies at Tenerife in Las Canarias.

I hoped to redeem myself by granting the crew a night's shore leave. My memory of the port was of a few poor shops and a selection of ill looking taverns that doubled as gaming dens and cat houses. Heaven for the men, I suppose. More than half of them cast off in row boats soon after we weighed anchor.

I didn't care to attract attention ashore by joining them. Instead, I watched through my telescope while the row boats docked in the harbour and the men leapt out in search of goods to buy and whores to board. After they had disappeared into the portside bustle, I turned to the table in my cabin. Jack Lance had drawn a route map a day into our voyage and I spent a half hour poring over it. Drawing out ink and pen, I wrote in the ship's journal that I kept, or rather made sporadic entries in.

3 o'clock. Docked at Tenerife port of Santa Cruz. Smooth seas for 3 days. Flynn to trade the damask if there's a fair price. Due to sail on 8 o'clock morning tide.

I put down the quill and rubbed my forefinger where the ink had stained it. Suddenly, I was acutely aware that Daniel was somewhere in the midship's cabins and there were hours ahead of us before we resumed sail. I could hear Flynn's voice ringing in my head now.

"He's an extra mouth to feed and an extra man to guard him."

He was right of course. Ditch him ashore or bring him to bed. Piss or get off the pot.

The cook's boy brought me supper. After all, I spent the night alone and Daniel stayed on board, in spite of his criticizing Queen Meg to her face. As I chewed a piece of bread, dunking it in wine to help the texture, I reflected that Daniel Stede might be the prisoner but I was bound too, caught between my own desire and the fear of acting on it. The cold chicken pie was dry in my mouth and the cheese too moist. The madeira went down well but even three cups of it failed to send me to a peaceful slumber.

CHAPTER 21

Sometime before dawn I woke to the noise of loud voices as the first boatload of carousing seamen arrived back on board. Someone brought out a fiddle and I listened as Pedlar and Jack Lance led the singing of a roundel. I had fallen asleep fully dressed, laid on the coverlet with only a shawl for the balmy night. I dressed my hair, painted my face and tied the shawl around me. After that, I climbed up the ladder to join the crew on deck. The song reminded me of the joys of my life at sea and I determined to throw off the rank, guilty mood I had sunk myself in. The men cheered when I appeared. I curtsied them and hallooed and even danced a jig with Gower, the men egging him on.

At the end of the tune, I noticed Daniel was there. Someone must have brought him up on deck for the air and entertainment. His lamp lit face watched me from the port side where he was tethered. I puzzled as to what his expression meant – desire fighting with disgust? Suddenly I didn't care to think about him any longer. I turned my back and sat down next to Flynn.

"Any news in port? Apart from your exploits with a whore or two, you can spare me that tale."

Flynn gave me a mock frown. I was glad to see the night ashore had lifted his ill-temper.

"Only one lady tonight, mistress, and she as fine as you might imagine. Hair like silk and beribboned garters that she showed very prettily."

"Only one jade? She must have been a beauty."

Flynn laughed. He was as drunk as most of them but he held his liquor well, a good trait for a ship's quartermaster.

"Truth is I spent most of the night at the gaming table, had a streak of the devil's good luck. But you'll be pleased with the stores we gathered, plenty to last us to the Antilles and beyond."

He paused and glanced around to make sure no one was listening. I was immediately on the alert.

"What, Flynn? You have some other news?"

"A Spanish seaman at the inn told me the Customs House in Malta was attacked by none other than the General."

I felt a chill run up my neck and pulled my shawl closer round me. The General was Black Hal's right hand man, when they weren't engaged in some argument or other.

"I thought he was still in Honduras, running a whorehouse of his own. Tell me what you heard about the General and the raid on the Customs House."

Flynn cupped a hand over my ear and spoke into it above another round of sea shanties.

"They say Black Hal tipped him off. In any case the General used firesticks to breach the Customs House and maim a couple of guards in the process. He got away with a rich haul, mostly coin and jewels from the Indies, then burned a few houses on the way back to the ship."

Bile rose in my throat. "Is he still in Malta?"

Flynn shrugged. "Not likely. He'll be skulking back to Honduras as fast as he can."

"Does he still sail that old bucket of a galleon?"

"The Sea Foam? I expect so."

I put my hands over my eyes and took a deep breath of the night air. I remembered the General's ship all too well. Wind and weather, wind and weather. I felt a breeze from the north, the one that had carried us smoothly. There was the thread of a cross current in it too.

"Flynn!" I threw up my head and gripped Flynn's warm calloused hand, startling him. "I'll ask Jack Lance to make the calculations but I'm almost certain I know which route the Sea Foam is bound to take. She was always a monster of a vessel but hard to manoeuvre on anything but strong and direct currents, and especially if she's laden."

"You can't mean to try an attack?"

"I do. We sail ahead of the morning tide, tack west by nor'west. With luck, we'll stitch our way to intercept Monsieur the General and relieve him of his fresh treasure."

"Ma'am, if you're thinking his boat will supply Conroy's money, I'd say it's more than doubtful."

I got to my feet, pulling Flynn up with me.

"I'm not thinking of Conroy. I'm thinking of teaching that scum of the sea a lesson he won't forget."

"Beg your pardon, ma'am, but the sooner we pay Conroy, the sooner we stop the danger of him sending government boats after us. Not to mention that Lord Stede may be planning the same. We need to deal with Conroy then disappear, fast."

I looked around at the men. Pedlar was the last singer, crooning a desultory rendering of 'Oceans deep and wide'. Joshua was drinking steadily with a couple of the new seamen while most of the others had drifted off to their hammocks or dozed where they sat.

The threat of being hounded by militia boats or worse, finding Black Hal on our tail, gripped me with panic. Damn them all, I wouldn't run and hide like a frightened animal. Fear gave way to rage, at Conroy, Stede, even Daniel, and especially Black Hal. I might have failed to beat Hal but here was a chance to hunt his vicious ally. Winning a fight with the General would send Hal a warning that Queen Meg was still a pirate to be reckoned with. Flynn was saying something but I shook my head and pointed at the sleeping men.

"Give them a couple of hours. Then we sail, full ahead and armed to the bows."

CHAPTER 22

The wind was behind us all the way. "A she-devil wind" Old Nick Masterton once called it. He was a navigator for nearly sixty years before he went mad, some say with the drink, others say witchcraft from the wife who loathed him. I had met him a score of times and he taught me a thing or two about marking the winds but mostly he told me to have faith in my own instinct.

"You've got the seeing eye for it. If you feel it on your skin, if you hear beyond the ocean's music then go with what you know, never mind if others think you've succumbed to sea madness."

That morning I wondered if Old Nick would have felt the sweet moment when we were atop the current and it tugged us neatly on course. I sensed it, as though my backbone lifted. I knew it as sure as day that we were crossing the line for the General's path from Malta. I sat quiet and comfortable on the fo'c'sle as the horizon turned from blue to purple and dusk began to fall. My fixation on chasing the General, or so Flynn called it, had turned my mind nicely away from guilt about Conroy or fear of Hal's pursuit and even my other obsession, Daniel. There's nothing like a pirate raid to lift the spirits and kick the blood into your veins.

Our boy on the main mast called out. "Sail! Sail, mistress!"

"What colour is it?"

I gazed up to see his slight frame swing this way and that. After a few minutes he called back. "Yellow, ma'am."

I clenched my fists in triumph. A dirty yellow sail and the caricature of a mermaid on the pennant – it was the General's galleon. I had been on board it enough times when I was in Hal's clutches. Back then the Sea Foam was cumbersome to sail and smelled rank, much like the General himself. Its clumsy bulk, however, made it difficult to broadside and the General had managed to defend it from many attacks. But even the most steadfast ship can only withstand so much and I intended to hit the Sea Foam with every piece of munition we possessed. Besides, we had the Night Wing's speed in our favour.

With the right timing we would plunge in, barrage the galleon and dart out again almost unscathed. We would be hit on the approach, of that I was certain, but with luck it would only be a shot or two of damage. The Sea Foam would be stopped in her tracks before she could gain on our retreat.

We had perhaps a half hour before we were lined up for the kill. I was restless as a cat so I ran to my cabin to change my clothes. This raid called for something especially dramatic. I wanted to give the General one clear message - death. I swapped my red tunic for a black fitted coat, added a black shawl and wide brimmed hat. Even the long plumed ostrich feathers were dyed ebony. I piled on necklaces of jet so that they glinted and jangled like anchor chains. Next, I added thick lines of kohl around my eyes and powdered my face and lips deathly white. The finishing touch was to knot my hair in a plait and pin a sheer black veil under the hat to denote widow's weeds.

Letting loose my excitement I flew up the ladder to arrive above deck. I was gratified by the dropped jaws of the men. They grasped the significance of the widow's garb right away. I spread my arms, turning slowly so all could see and hear me.

"Spare no quarter today! This marks the end of the General and a blow to his crony, Black Hal. We'll turn his precious Sea Foam into scrap and booty!"

I strode to the fo'c'sle and placed my hand on Flynn's shoulder as he shifted us on course for a direct hit at the galleon. The Sea Foam bore down on us and I nerved myself to stay where I was even when they let loose the first cannon shot. It ripped across our foredeck, taking two of my men in its wake. The Sea Foam's next shot slashed the corner of our mainsail, not enough to throw us but unnerving nonetheless.

I drew my cutlass and pointed it steady towards the prow of our opponent's ship. I could see the General's men scurrying everywhere and the shift of the cannons as they reloaded. A molten ball of fire-shot beat across our deck, setting ropes ablaze and narrowly missing Catter and two other men. They set to dousing the flame right away though black smoke billowed up, choking the air. I hoped the blaze misled the

General into believing he'd wreaked more damage than he had.

One, two breaths and we were in range. I slashed my cutlass through the air to signal the attack.

"Now!"

My men offered no warning sally but hit the galleon with a barrage of every cannon, firestick, makeshift shot of rusty nails and iron bars that we could muster. We kept up the assault without pause, bearing down on the Sea Foam until we were close enough to smell their burning sails. The wind blew the smoke in tattered wreaths. As the black clouds parted we saw carnage everywhere on their deck. The ferocity of our unflinching attack had completely blindsided them. With all my intuition, even I had not expected to break their main mast and send it kicking like a wounded dog across their deck, dragging sails and ropes and men with it.

Suddenly I saw him, a figure on the prow, the General. There was no mistaking him. He wore his customary green jacket and a black tri-cornered hat as though he was a real military man and not the lying knave he had always been. I raced to the ship's side to get as close as I could to him, screaming at the top of my lungs.

"You're done for! The next time you meet Black Hal will be in hell!"

A white pennant fluttered from amidships and flapped its way up the second mast like a broken bird. Jack Lance, standing at the port side, pointed up and shouted.

"They've surrendered!" He turned to me, a disbelieving expression on his face. "The General's bloody well surrendered – take him, mistress!"

The white pennant fluttered across my vision, its purity taunting me, reminding me of the pirate's code of honour. A picture of Hal flashed through my mind and an instinct to murder along with it.

"No! No surrender! No quarter!"

Cal shouted from the fo'c'sle. He turned and cupped a hand at his mouth to call to the men. "Throw the grapple hooks."

I ran. As soon as the first hooks went across and the ropes were secure I was among the first to swarm over. As I leapt on board the Sea Foam, I advanced on the General, my cutlass unsheathed. He should have bowed his head or had the good sense to keep the sneering twist of his mouth from me. I ran him through before he drew another breath. The sneer was replaced by a look of surprise then horror as he coughed the blood and life out of his lungs. I pulled the cutlass blade from his chest and he fell to the deck.

I leapt past him and hacked the pennant rope. The white cloth fluttered down and I caught it neatly on my bloodstained blade. All I could see was Hal's taunting, pitiless face when he first kidnapped me. Swinging round on my men as they jumped on deck I gave a blood chilling scream.

"No mercy and no quarter!"

I leapt to the side and scrambled across the ropes back to the Night Wing. The noise of carnage and butchery filled my ears, a cacophony straight from hell itself. A girl's scream cut through the din and I swung around to see a female prisoner being herded out of the Sea Foam's hold and on to the deck. Horrified, I tried to call out an order to spare her. My words were drowned in a terrible cracking sound. There was no hope for her or any prisoners trapped below. The Seam Foam keeled, her deck piked in the centre and water rushed in, forcing the timbers further apart. I heard screams and Flynn shouting over the chaos.

"Abandon ship!"

My men hauled themselves across the dipping and spinning ropes, carrying boxes and sacks of booty and hurling themselves clear of the sinking ship. Joshua, Pedlar and Gower hacked at the grapple lines to free the Night Wing from the Sea Foam's last death throes. She went under at a frightening speed. I stayed on the fo'c'sle, gripped with the aftershock of horror. Dusk clouds gathered and the light faded on a score of drowning men. We sped away at full sail. Behind us, the relic of the Sea Foam's main mast and the rest of her treasure sank to the bottom of the sea.

CHAPTER 23

In a daze, I retreated to my cabin. I sat on my unmade bed then paced and sat again. struggling to take stock of what I'd done. It was Cal who appeared at my cabin door to tell me the reckoning. He gave a start when he saw me close up in the black clothes and hat, the kohl and white makeup smeared on my face.

"Where's Flynn?" I said.

"He's busy organizing help for the survivors, ma'am."

He kept his eyes down and his hands clasped together in front of him.

"Too busy to speak to me, then?"

"Beg pardon, milady."

Perhaps it was for the best. I didn't relish seeing more disappointment or judgement in Flynn's eyes. I had proven myself the worst of pirates. Even Black Hal honoured a surrender flag, though he would exact revenge later. I stood up and reached for a cup and jug. My hands shook.

"Pour me some rum, would you, Cal? And for yourself."

Cal filled my cup and handed it to me, though still not meeting my eyes. He took none for himself. I sipped, barely able to swallow. The liquid tasted acrid, of smoke and pitch, the scent that still clung everywhere since we'd wrenched the Night Wing clear of the dying Sea Foam.

"Only two of our men dead, ma'am, and the crow's nest boy, Jamie Bellock." I nodded dumbly. Cal drew a breath and went on. "At the last count we had twelve casualties, one of them not like to last the night. Pat Fenwick took a cannon shot in the shoulder blade. The surgeon can't do more than keep him unconscious for the pain."

I bit my lip and waited.

"Only six survivors from the Sea Foam, milady. Flynn reckons we got about half the booty before she went down. Maybe enough to pay Master Conroy, though."

My fingers reached out across the table, smoothing the edge of the parchment map, touching a dried sea anemone that held my quills, coming back to the smooth cup. My hands were like birds, seemingly unattached to me.

"Thank you Cal."

"Are we back on course for the Antilles, ma'am?"

"Yes, Cal, back on course."

He turned and quietly left the cabin. I stared at the closed door, my blue coat hanging there as usual, swaying gently on its hook. I had the strongest urge to visit Daniel, to search his eyes for the revulsion that surely must be there. At least another pirate would know that the firm tradition of accepting surrender would still likely end in a few deaths. It was usual that the conquering ship held a makeshift trial and often executed prisoners. But to a man from the ordinary world of peace and order, a man like Daniel, all they would see me for was an out and out murderer.

The cabin suddenly felt stifling but I couldn't bear to go to the window and let in a breeze. Along with the fresh salt tang would be the smell of cannon shot and deck fire. My chest was already choked with it. Taking off my hat I crossed to the hanging glass to unpick the remains of the black veil. I gasped with shock at my reflection. It was no wonder Cal wouldn't look at me. My face and mouth were chalk white and the kohl had smudged enourmous black circles around my eyes. I truly was a death's head and with a score of men's lives on my soul. I stared for a long time at the skull-like face that glared back at me.

"Hal's daughter," I said.

I bathed and bathed, scrubbed my face and hair and bathed again. Poor Joshua was called to carry six buckets until I was satisfied I had obliterated all traces of that black death witch. Digging through my clothes chest I found an orange taffeta dress, more suited for a garden party than a sea voyage. I added a turquoise scarf as a bandana around my unpinned hair. Feeling naked without makeup and hat I donned a Venetian eye mask, jeweled with blue stones and tied with a gold ribbon.

I rarely ate below decks with the men so their expressions ranged from surprise to shock and in some cases pleasure when I appeared. It took all my nerve to show myself after the attack but I had to replace that ghoulish image of myself with something more fetching, as much for their morale as mine. I stooped my head under the low timbers and squeezed in next to Gower to sit at one of the long tables.

"What's supper tonight, boys?" I spoke jovially, sticking my dagger blade down in the table top. The cook on duty hurried to serve me with a heaped plate.

"Chicken, milady, and ship's bread for the gravy."

"I don't see the bread. Is it so full of weevils it can walk to the table by itself?"

The cook looked stricken so I had to laugh myself to show him it was a bad joke. I felt the men relax a little. Catter raised his beaker of rum in a toast.

"To the General, may he never rise from the seven seas' depth to blight more lives."

It was a solemn oath for a conquered enemy and I was grateful to Catter. He had dignified my actions and reminded us all that, white flag or not, the General had been one of the most evil villains on the ocean. The men murmured in unison.

"Seven seas' depth."

There was a restrained clinking of cups then Jack Lance called out.

"Pedlar, how about a song?"

Pedlar bobbed his carrot-haired head up from the next table and nodded to me.

"If you'll allow me a mouthful of meat and grog to wet my whistle, ma'am."

I waved a gracious hand and attended to my own supper. The chicken was stringy but surprisingly flavoursome. One of the ship's boys lit a couple more lamps that warmed the under deck with their steady glow. Taking another forkful of chicken I glanced up to see Daniel, escorted by Flynn, standing next to the cook's pot to snack on their supper.

"Master Stede." He did a double take when he saw me amongst the men in all my finery. "You don't seem plagued with the sickness these days. Have you found your sea legs?"

"It's been a smooth voyage and I believe I am more accustomed to the ship's motion."

For a long moment I could have fancied us in another life, talking in a drawing room somewhere. I remembered evenings from my childhood when I would listen to grownups speaking nicely together. Daniel broke the spell with his next remark.

"Apart from the bloody sea battle, of course."

His sarcasm was a direct insult. I laughed heartily to cover it and some of the men joined in. But I felt chilled at the sight of Daniel's tight mouth and jaw, showing for all the world his loathing of my murderous actions. Moments later his gaze slipped sidelong at mine and there I saw it again, fleeting but uncontrollable and unmistakable - desire. Blood rushed to my face as my answering passion pushed aside the spectre of death and guilt at the massacre. This was what I needed, this would make me whole, passion and life, not useless wallowing in self-loathing and remorse.

"Are you a gambling man, Master Stede?"

"No, I can't say I am."

"But you can hold a game of cards surely, piquet, bezique?"

The memory of drawing rooms had brought with it a pleasant picture of learning card games with my father on cold evenings by our fire-lit hearth.

"Yes, I can manage a hand of piquet."

"It's settled then. Joshua, you and Flynn and Master Stede may join me in my cabin after supper to while away the evening with a few rounds of four hand."

I stood up to squeeze my way around the men. Some of them tried to rise at my departure but I gestured them to stay seated.

"Good night boys. Queen Meg thanks you for your loyalty today."

The words almost choked me. I'd put them through a battle that should never have ended as it did but they murmured and nodded as I made my way out and I knew my instinct to face them and make merry had been a good one.

CHAPTER 24

Flynn and Joshua didn't even feign surprise when I dismissed them.

"I've decided the card game will be a two-hander after all."

Flynn rolled his eyes. I pretended I hadn't noticed. I closed the door after them then turned to Daniel. He was standing, watchful, in the middle of the cabin. I had pictured him here many times and now I had him. I wondered at the skittishness that had held me back for so long. Such coyness seemed like the act of a foolish girl, not Queen Meg.

"Take a seat."

He sat down in one of the two upright chairs at the table. I stepped around him to take the other chair opposite. I placed a hand on his back as I passed, feeling his warmth under the loose fabric of his shirt. Once I was seated and facing him I untied the ribbons of the eye mask and placed it decoratively on a book that was laid open by my hand. He didn't speak or look at me. I put my feet up on the table, leaned back and regarded him.

"No cards?" Daniel said.

"No cards. I thought we would play something more interesting. Let's start with a guessing game."

"I have a question to guess at. Why do you keep me here when it's obvious my father will never pay you a ransom?"

"Perhaps I hold out hope that Lord Stede is a decent, caring fellow or perhaps I have plans to sell you elsewhere."

I saw the beat of a pulse in his throat where his shirt lay open. He frowned and his tongue wet his mouth as, discomfited, he avoided my eyes and tried to think of a response. I stared until he couldn't help but lift his gaze to mine. The atmosphere thickened. I felt the excitement of my own desire and my imminent conquest.

I got to my feet and took four measured paces to where Daniel sat. Clutching the front of his shirt I dragged him to standing and fastened my mouth on his. His lips parted in shock, then we were kissing with a passion and frenzy unmatched by my imagination. Wrenching his jacket off his shoulders, I slid my hands across the smooth shirt and the curve of his chest beneath. He gasped then pushed me off him so hard I fell against the table. I gripped the edge of it to steady myself. Daniel had his back turned to me, one hand covering his face.

"Why do you fight me?" I said. "You obviously want me."

"God help me, I do."

"Then let us be together, and there's an end to it."

When he swung around to face me, I started at the mingled expression of pain and grief in his face.

"I quarrelled with my father before I left to go overseas. It's been more than two years and I never made my peace with him. You kidnapped me before I could stand face to face with him again."

He lurched sideways as the Night Wing rode a sudden swell then righted herself again. The lamp light flickered. For a second its shadows mimicked the black outline of the General's ship and its tattered, broken masts. I forced away the memory of it, wanting to feast my gaze on Daniel, not be haunted by dark spectres.

"You will see your father again. Have some adventures with me first then I'll take you home to visit. Do you know what I've been thinking?"

"No, and I'm damned if I can make you out at all."

"I think we make a fine pair, you and I."

Daniel looked at me, incredulous. I smiled at him and smoothed my skirt.

"I wasn't always like this. I was a gentleman's daughter, brought up to be a lady, educated, like you."

"I can see that, but why this?"

Daniel gestured at the cabin, my outlandish dress.

"That's a story for another time." I was suddenly filled with cold dread that I might blurt out the story of Hal and my abduction. The black chasm inside me threatened to yawn wider than the jaws of hell.

"Are you a witch, as some men call you? Is that what you've done to me, placed me under an evil charm?"

I hit him full across the face. My hand stung and I clenched a fist, ready to strike again. Rage. I welcomed it, far better than the precarious grief that had just threatened.

"Are you like all the rest? You men can't even claim your own lust but have to put the blame on a woman for bewitching you."

Daniel had the grace to look shame-faced.

"You're right, I'm trying to find an excuse for how I feel."

He took a step towards me and touched my arm lightly.

"You have shaken everything I've ever known or wanted. I don't know how I conjured these feelings towards you. Perhaps they're born out of frustration and not knowing my fate. In any case, I beg your pardon."

"Oh, all the gentleman now."

"My father doesn't think so. He says I have a touch of the peasant about me because I try to help our farmers. I refuse to play the autocrat and it puts us at odds." He glanced up and smiled. "He would have apoplexy if he saw me now, conversing with a beautiful female pirate."

I don't know who took a step first but I found myself leaning my body against his tall frame, sliding my hands around his waist, cradling my head against his chest. He put both his arms around me and buried his face in my hair. I felt him exhale, the sigh of a man who has fallen in the sea's strong current and at last given up the fight against drowning. God knows how I controlled myself but I kissed his cheek and spoke softly.

"Perhaps this is enough for now. We have some peace between us and I'm glad for it."

"Peace? I'm more in turmoil than ever."

His hands gripped me tightly then abruptly he pushed me away, wrenched open the cabin door and was gone.

I didn't move, overwhelmed as I was by the tenderness that had arisen between us. His lust I had been sure of but not this passionate feeling. A wave of fear took me. Carefully I tamped it down and concentrated on the conquest I had made tonight. Not yet consummated but for now it was enough to know I had Daniel in my grasp. I had breached the wall of his better judgement and gentlemanly instincts. Queen Meg had won the day.

CHAPTER 25

For the next four days I made no move towards Daniel except for a nod of acknowledgement, a pause and a warm smile when I passed him on deck. He burned for me, I could see that, and God knows I ached for him. We were a week out from Cartagena and calm seas still favoured us. I kept to my cabin that day, nestled amongst cushions on the seat below my window, my eyes skimming the pages of a book on Spanish history, my imagination dancing with visions of Daniel's fair countenance.

Over and again I replayed the glance he'd given me, his desire naked in his eyes. It was a moment to treasure like a rare jewel. I believe I kept myself away from him for fear of tarnishing it. I snapped the book shut and cursed myself for a coward. Where was Meg's bravado now? Let him taste you, I heard her whisper, and he'll be thirstier still.

I leapt to my feet and left the cabin. I found Joshua amidships, teaching one of the ship's boys how to play dice. He stood up and greeted me, keeping his head bowed under the low timbers.

The boy followed suit, staring at me wide-eyed.

"What's the matter, boy?" I said. "You've never seen a ship's captain before?"

"Not close, ma'am. And not so pretty."

I couldn't have wished to hear a better compliment that day so I leaned forward and kissed the boy's cheek. He smelled of candle grease and the carbolic Flynn made them bathe in.

"What's your name?"

"Benjamin Heaton, ma'am."

"Well, Benjamin, run and tell the cook I'd like an early supper for two served in my cabin."

Weaving between the low slung hammocks, he ran off to the cook's stove. I turned to Joshua, though I couldn't meet his eye.

"Bring the prisoner to me at the same time as the meal."

Joshua knew better than to voice an opinion one way or another. I almost asked him what the men thought of me keeping Daniel on board after I had to failed to extract a ransom for him. As long as they believed Queen Meg had found a pretty plaything I was content. Even Flynn, who had a nose for these things, must never suspect I was truly smitten.

I withdrew to my cabin to draw the curtains and light the lamps, even though it was an hour shy of twilight. I couldn't decide what to wear then settled for the crimson dress with a pale blue gown worn as a robe unbuttoned on top of it. To pass the time I laid out my collection of combs and hair clasps then selected half a dozen of the most ornate and secured my hair in a tumble of curls. After my toilet I cleared the table of all but a few choice books and the decanter of madeira. Flitting to and fro across the cabin I caught sight of my earnest, frowning expression in the glass. It brought me up short. I spoke to my reflection.

"Is this what it's come to? Trying to impress the spoiled son of a lord with your books and best silks?"

I pulled a face at myself then started at a rap on the door. I opened it to find the duty cook had brought the supper tray himself. He had made a fine job of it, platters of fruit and cold cuts, warm biscuits, dried fish and, in pride of place, two boiled eggs fresh laid from our last chickens. I nodded my approval and he placed the tray at one end of the table. He made a great fuss of it, trying to pour out the wine before I asked and staring about my cabin so openly I had to shoo him out.

Almost half an hour later, Joshua fetched Daniel. They had made an obvious effort to clean him up. He was freshly bathed, his hair in a neat ribbon, his shirt new laundered. He must have felt like a prize pig brought to market. His scowling expression betrayed his anger. I avoided his glare, told myself his rage would add spice and sent Joshua on his way. I gestured at the banquet of food.

"Eat something, anything you like."

"You all but ignored me for four days. What do you want?"

"A pleasant supper. Conversation."

"What have we to say to each other that won't disgrace us both?"

I controlled an urge to shout at him for his ill manners.

"Come, Daniel, we have another week's sailing before we reach harbour. Can we not pass the time pleasantly?"

"For God's sake! How long do you wish to toy with me?"

The hurt in his voice panicked me. When I had him in my fantasies there was none of this to deal with, his vivid face, his pleading expression, the complications of a human being with his own mind and will. The cabin felt claustrophobic, heavy with the smell of fruit and wine. I reached out a hand. He jerked backwards then in two strides was at the door. As he grabbed for the handle, I had my dagger at his neck. The panic left me. This I understood, violence and mutiny. Daniel leaned against the door, his shoulders slumped in a despairing gesture. I sheathed the dagger in my belt and placed a hand on his arm. I spoke harshly.

"Go back to your cabin if you must."

He looked down at my hand still resting on the warm wool of his jacket. I slid it away but he took hold of it and turned it over to kiss my palm. The gesture was so simple, so heartfelt, that it took the breath out of me. He kissed my wrist then I was in his arms and the kisses were on my mouth, neck, breast. It was as thought we had been perched on top of the rapids and were suddenly tipped over in a downward plunge.

"Meg," he said.

My hands dragged at his clothes until the jacket was cast aside and the linen shirt pulled open. His mouth at my breast had me arching with pleasure and we stumbled backwards to the table, scattering books aside. A glass or bottle, I know not which, crashed to the floor. Daniel's hands were under my skirt, the fine fingers I had imagined touching me so many times were cool as silk on my burning skin.

I don't know if it was the scorched smell of a fly caught in the lantern or the fluttering curtain against the night sky but my mind was suddenly whipped back to an unbidden memory. I was fourteen, my house ablaze and Hal's grimy paw clutching my arm. Of course I knew it was Daniel's body over me, his smooth muscled chest and stomach sliding against mine. My hands touched his flushed face and silken hair but another part of myself was being cast adrift on nightmare memories of other men who had lain with me, the first and worst being Black Hal.

I kicked and flailed away from him.

"Meg, what is it?"

Daniel's voice roared in my ears like the ocean. I would have screeched and climbed the walls like a cat if I'd been able. Instead, I grabbed his coat and shirt from the floor and threw it at him.

"Meg."

I couldn't speak. I was afraid that if I opened my mouth something terrible would come out of it.

"Are you ill? Should I get help?"

I shook my head violently. I felt ice cold. Daniel tried to embrace me as I backed away. Terror swamped me. I yanked the loaded musket from the shelf behind the door and pointed it at his chest. My hands were shaking. Daniel looked frightened but beyond that, I saw his concern for me.

"Get out," I said.

I believe it was my look of desperate pleading more than the firearm that sent Daniel reluctantly from the cabin.

I held the musket at firing point for a long time after the door closed behind him. Heat and sweat rushed back through my body and my finger slipped wet on the hard metal trigger. I walked to the door and carefully slid the bolt across. Hal can't get in now, I told the terrified girl inside me. I climbed into bed, cradling the musket, and pulled the blankets tight around my shoulders. For the longest time, I listened to every tiny scraping sound above deck and below, every creak and nudge of the ship until I knew it was my own dear Night Wing rocking beneath me. My body relaxed and I could breathe again, one breath then another, into sleep.

CHAPTER 26

I woke as the first sun rays slid between the half closed drapes. The memory of the previous night was waiting, coiled like a snake, ready to strike. I rolled out of bed to escape it. Throwing a splash of tepid water on my face, I dressed as quickly as I could. I didn't choose silk and bodices today but clothed myself in man's trousers and jerkin. I caked my face with makeup, tied a scarlet bandana around my forehead and jammed a tri-cornered hat on top of it.

Before I went on deck, I had to make sure of one thing. Strapping my sword belt around my hips, I readied myself and slid the bolt free on the cabin door. Glancing outside, I spied one of the ship's boys disappearing up the stairs, his bare feet splayed one by one on the ladder's rungs.

"Look below!" I said.

He came scurrying back down and stood to attention before me.

"Tam, isn't it?"

He tucked his chin and smiled, pleased I knew his name.

"Run and find Joshua. Tell him the prisoner should be kept below today and not to let him out until after dark. Understand?"

Tam nodded and ran off to do as I bid. I shut my door again and breakfasted on the supper Daniel and I should have eaten the night before, perhaps fed to each other in the love nest of my bed. I could have shouted with pain. I wanted Daniel more than ever, but I saw no way of bringing it about. I was truly what Hal had made me. How could I ever erase it, or look Daniel in the face again.? I wondered what he thought of me now, a lunatic at the least. I remembered the concern in his eyes even when I had held the musket to his chest. Last night we had both seen what damaged goods Queen Meg really was.

It burned like a fever that Hal still had this terrible power over me. It was unbearable. I felt myself slip towards the edge of panic again. I had to fight him, there had to be a way. The thought of putting Daniel off at the next port and never seeing him again was too much to bear. Suddenly, a plan appeared, as clear as my schemes for changing course. At first it seemed ridiculous even to my fevered mind but little by little, I decided it was the only solution. Daniel and I must marry. A sanctified union would surely drive away the ghost of Hal and my terrible past. A proper wedding was fitting for the lady Daniel deserved. He may object at first but he would come to see it was the only way for us. I would not be destroyed by this. Rather, I would give myself to a man of my own choosing, and in the sight of God, assuming God hadn't abandoned me long ago.

I ate methodically to give Joshua time to carry out my orders before running up to the main deck. Cal was at the wheel while Joshua sat cross-legged with Cameron on the deck behind, playing some combination of dice and cards. Everyone was taking advantage of the ease from duties thanks to our plain sailing. Flynn was nowhere to be seen. Cal greeted me.

"Morning, mistress."

Joshua looked up and caught my eye.

"Ma'am, the prisoner asked to speak to you."

He kept his expression blank, and I was sure Daniel's gentlemanly manners wouldn't have betrayed anything that had passed between us. Even so, I felt a blush creep into my face.

"Daniel's sea sickness has eased but he still doesn't do so well being kept below," Joshua said. "I think he's heartily tired of the ocean."

"Yes, I daresay."

I glanced up at the blazing sky. The thick fabric of my trousers itched. Sweat pooled on my neck. Flynn appeared from below and raised a hand in greeting.

"Just out of bed, Quartermaster?"

He pretended to look injured.

"I've been counting the booty we took from the General's ship, ma'am."

"A good haul?"

"Very. If we make a fair trade on the jewels there'll be plenty to pay off the shipwright and a few doubloons over."

"That's good news and I thank you for it. Trade we will. Hugh Catter can do the deal when we reach Cartagena."

I felt a weight lifted off me. At least the debt to Conroy would be paid.

"Buy Conroy a new coat into the bargain. Recompense for the couple of nights we had to lock him up. It's a relief not to raid my own treasure store."

"Will we sail back to Scotland right away?" Cal said.

I shook my head.

"Cameron, when we reach Cartagena I want you to take a handful of men and book a passage back to Scotland. I'm sending you as peace envoy to Conroy and to square my debts."

"Happy to, ma'am."

Shielding my eyes, I turned a circle to take in the curve of the horizon. The smell of rotten fish caught my throat. I wrinkled my nose and took in the sight of Gower who was standing with a line at the portside. The stench was coming from a pile of fish scraps at his feet.

"What in God's name is Gower about?"

"Using old fish to catch the new," Joshua said.

"Tell him to heave that bilge over the side and mind he doesn't go in after it."

"Talking of heaving things over the side, we should put the prisoner ashore when we reach Cartagena," Flynn said.

I glanced at him and saw the meaning in his expression. Flynn knew all was not well with me and Master Stede and that a moping ship's captain was of no use to anyone. He spoke again, with more firmness than was necessary.

"He needs to feel firm land again and we need to trim our load."

"Dry land is what he'll get." Suddenly, I had my plan. "We all will. Flynn, I intend to set up house north of Cartagena, in one of those nice green valleys I remember from our last trip there."

"Set up house? You, ma'am?"

"You can urge all you like, but I've thought of another way to tap Lord Stede's pocket. If he won't cough up the money I ask for, I intend to marry his son. He can have a pirate queen for a daughter and see how he likes that for a ransom."

"You played the game with Lord Stede and lost, ma'am, if you don't mind my saying so."

"I do mind. Queen Meg never loses, and it will be Lady Stede to you. With a new home and a reprieve from the ocean, Daniel will come to enjoy his new life."

Flynn frowned and walked off without a word. I'd never seen him so put out, or the effort it took him to hold his tongue. So be it. They would all learn to like it or go packing. I was shaking at my own audacity but the more I thought of it the more I warmed to the idea. Surely Daniel would appreciate being given his own house far away from his father's controlling reach. I felt the ghosts of my past smothered in the excitement of my scheme. I was sure this was how Daniel and I could be brought together as we should. I looked up at the mains'l. The sky arced above in a dome of pure blue. It would be fine sailing all the way to the Caribbean.

CHAPTER 27

It's hard for any pirate to dock in Cartagena without the dragoons or the Customs walking all over you. What you need is a network of trustworthy and discreet bodyguards and scouts. Thanks to Cal, that's exactly what we had. Two of Cal's brothers were natives of the place so they and a brace of cousins ensured the Night Wing and crew were safely stowed from prying eyes.

The whole voyage, I had thought about nothing else except my scheme to marry Daniel. One small part of my mind wondered if I had been unhinged by the memories evoked by Daniel touching me that night. I had avoided him since but the more I dwelled on it the more I was determined to have him, be with him, in spite of the spectre of Black Hal. A sacred marriage would lay the ghosts of my dark past and bind me and Daniel together, safe and forever. I knew my chances of finding another man as fine as him were slim to none. I might be cursed as Hal's whore forever more, and that I could not allow.

Meanwhile, Hugh Catter haggled a good price on the General's bounty of jewels, aided by a reluctant Joshua who was worrying again about someone recognising him, though who he thought would know him as a poacher so far from England I couldn't imagine. I was delighted with the outcome. I would be able to pay off the crew, settle my debt to Conroy and, most importantly, fund a wedding and furnish a bridal house.

After arranging for the Night Wing to be cleaned and overhauled, I saw Cameron off on the first leg of his voyage back to Scotland. As I shook his hand and watched him secure Conroy's gold under his coat, I noticed Flynn and Catter watching with approval. Everyone, myself included, was relieved to discharge that dishonourable debt. I reflected with gratitude that I still had a few truly loyal men. Wedding or no, it would be good to give us all a few weeks of peace on shore and far away from the memories of Cornwall.

I was escorted to Cal's eldest brother's house in the hills, along with Flynn, Gower, Pedlar and Cal himself. On my orders they brought Daniel with us. Long rays from the afternoon sun lit the horizon as we made our way out of the port and climbed into the hills. The men were on horseback while I travelled in a covered wagon. Gower stayed at the rear of the party in case any spies had latched on to our little group. I lay back on the seat cushions and did my best to relax against the motion of the carriage, sharp and jolting after the easy swing of the Night Wing.

The further we travelled from the ocean, the more anxious I became. I put it down to nerves about Daniel and rehearsed in my head how I would broach my plan to him. I must have dozed because the carriage stopped what seemed like minutes later. I waited until Cal opened the door and let down the steps for me to alight. He looked full of happy anticipation to be seeing his family again. I felt a stab of envy that that would never be me.

"All safe and sound, ma'am."

I threw a shawl around my head and shoulders and took in the view of a charming white mansion house. It had been much improved since Cal's family first secured it, in exchange for hiding us from Customs and robber gangs alike.

"So, this is what our bribe money can buy."

"Yes, ma'am, and my brothers are grateful for it."

The eldest, Marcel, stepped from the open doorway and held out a hand in greeting. He was very like Cal to look at, though more thickset and with a comfortable sense about him that contrasted with Cal's sharp restlessness. I shook his hand graciously.

"It's been at least three years since we enjoyed your hospitality."

He bowed.

"Always a pleasure." He turned to Cal and said, in Spanish, "I sent Lilian and the children to their grandmother. They're at an age where they're curious about everything."

"What about the servants?" Cal said.

"I've given them a few days holiday. We'll have to manage between us, brother. But there's plenty of food and clean linen."

I interrupted him. "Speaking of that, I'm more than ready for a bath and a change of clothes."

Marcelo led the way through the square entrance hall to the rear of the house. The last rays of sun filled the windows and traced a filigree pattern through the half closed shutters. I liked the sense of ease the house gave off. The warm adobe walls, pale shutters, simple furniture and colourful rugs and cushions were as pleasing as could be.

My room, at the corner of the house, was small. The bed almost filled it, once you squeezed in a washstand and painted chair. I liked it. It reminded me of my cabin on board the Night Wing, especially when Marcelo lit a lantern against the gathering dusk.

"We'll dine in an hour, if that suits you, madam. We killed a pig yesterday so there's good fresh meat. I set out the table on the back verandah. We have a pleasant view over the orchard and out to the hills."

"I look forward to it."

With that happy notion, Marcelo left me to bathe and rest, or rather to bathe and fret on what I would say to Daniel. My headstrong plan now seemed preposterous. I was astonished at how my mood could dip and soar by turns. I was gripped with a realisation that I had no idea what Daniel thought of me since that disastrous night. It surely was nothing good. The only thing that gave me hope was the passion he had shown me.

Pedlar knocked on my door and deposited a chest of my belongings. I opened it and immediately regretted not packing more clothes. I had left most of them in my cabin, intending to buy more, in view of my fresh start. After laying everything out on the bed I chose a white dress and all the gold and scarlet I could find – shawls, bracelets, silk slippers, beads and combs. After dressing, I regarded myself in the small glass and realised with a shock that I had no style at all. Nothing I wore matched or was understated like the dresses of the elegant ladies I'd see around the ports.

I frowned and threw off some of the jewellery then put it back on again. It was hopeless. Not for the first time, I considered that I had lacked a mother in that critical time when a teenage girl was helped to grow into a woman. Black Hal had dressed me like his painted doll then when I was free of him I became a magpie, gathering every gaudy thing I could find. Perhaps my collection of clothes gave me something to hang on to when I had lost everything else.

I shook off that maudlin thought, blaming my infatuation with Daniel for even considering such things. Adding another shawl, I buckled my sword belt over it for good measure. I had scrubbed my face clean but now my naked visage made me feel too exposed. I spent a half hour painting my eyes and lips and dressing my hair with metres of gold ribbon. A ring on every finger and thumb completed the effect. By the time I was done I had gone from defiant to sorrow and back again. Daniel wanted me, even if it was for lust. I hoped his passion was enough to achieve my purpose. It seemed that even in love I was a pirate. There was no point pretending otherwise.

CHAPTER 28

At last I stepped out to the candle lit hall. The wide rear door had been opened to reveal the table set as Marcelo had promised. The men, including Pedlar, Stanmore, Flynn and Gower, were seated around it, their faces rosy in the lamp light. Marcelo was serving platters of food. He saw me hovering in the doorway and gestured, smiling, for me to take my seat at the centre of the table.

"This is our brother Luis," he said. He gestured towards a younger version of himself who was helping carry dishes.

Luis glanced up and stared at my garish costume. It pleased me to see that familiar reaction, shock mingled with lust and a dash of fear writ in his eyes and slack jaw.

"Luis lives close by on his own farm and is to be married next month," Cal said.

I lifted an empty cup to toast the happy event and Cal quickly poured me a measure of wine. As I drank, my gaze lingered on Daniel where he sat at the far end of the table. His face was in shadow and unreadable. I took my seat and ate, laughed and caroused with the men. They enjoyed themselves, their sea stories and jests more raucous as the meal went on. Daniel said little and ate less. My hope that he

would be full of wine and amiable by the night's end shrank
to nought.

Luis' bride-to-be appeared to help with serving. Seeing the
couple's open affection for each other did nothing to lift my
mood. To cover my dismay, I was as gay and lively as could
be. Soon I was properly in my cups, the worse for drink that I
had ever been since I escaped Black Hal. The lamplight
flickered, the moon swayed in the sky as the night scents
thickened around us. Cal uncorked a fresh bottle of madeira.

"You've kept this cellared a long time," Pedlar said. "I
remember these bottles from our last visit."

"Only because you were too sick to drink any of it," Flynn
observed. "Some plague you'd picked up when we put in at
Port Lombard."

Gower chimed in. "A sickly squib, that's what I called you."
He banged the table with the flat of his hand. "But you came
good, a good buccaneer, none better."

He held out his cup to be refilled, quaffed it in one draft and
we all followed suit. The madeira was silken fruit in my
mouth. I stumbled to my feet and lifted my cup.

"Good buccaneers all! A toast to pirates everywhere!"

"Except Black Hal, damn his evil soul," Flynn said.

"And the General, all gone now, gone now to the deep." Pedlar said, turning his remark into a refrain.

The more I drank the more I stared at Daniel, fixated on my plan for him. Still, he would barely look at me. I stood up and made my unsteady way to the end of the table where he sat, morose.

"Aren't you drinking with us, sir?"

"I've drunk enough."

I sat down heavily in his lap. He flinched then slid his hands around my waist. Pedlar whistled. I gave Marcelo a wink.

"This gentleman is my guest, though I wish him to be more."

I paused to consider if my speech was slurred. Marcelo nodded as though he understood me so I carried on.

"Mr Daniel Stede and me, our paths are entwined, one with the other. It is our fate and that's the fact of it."

Cal snorted a laugh. "Fate and on account of us kidnapping him from Plymouth."

I scowled at him. "Master Luis! Tell us where you are to marry." Before he could do so I put my arms around Daniel's neck and said, "Because I have a fancy to tie the knot myself."

I was dimly aware that everyone had fallen silent.

"It seems you're a lucky man, Mister Stede," Marcelo said.

Gower banged on the table again.

"Queen Meg's the finest prize on the seven seas!"

There were more toasts and shouting. Daniel's voice cut through the din. "She is very fine. But I am her kidnapped prisoner who she has used badly from start to finish. Yet I find myself bewitched and there's my dilemma, gentlemen. I'd like to hear how you'd answer it."

"You think me fine?" I said.

"You know I do."

I stopped his mouth with a kiss. There was a ripple of applause and uneasy laughter. Flynn broke the tense moment.

"You're a handsome couple, there's no mistaking that."

I pulled back from the kiss to search Daniel's eyes and saw in them what my heart desired. He still yearned for me. I nestled closer and put my head on his shoulder.

Marcelo laughed. "I fail to see any dilemma here, Mister Stede."

"Daniel, will you marry me?" I sounded stupid with drink.

"Meg, don't be foolish." No one had called me Meg since I ran away from Hal's clutches. "There's no life for us together. This a drunken whim."

"No! I've thought on it for days. It's not a whim."

"Of course it is. Everything's a whim for you. You're extraordinary and beautiful and God knows I'm a besotted fool. But what did you think? That I shall run away and be a pirate with you? You've used me ill, Meg. I'm not a toy you can pick up and cast off as you please."

I heard my voice as a pleading wail. "I have! I used you very ill, but I won't make you be a pirate. I have another plan. Marcelo will find us a house and we'll be man and wife together as other people are."

"Oh Meg, I'm stupidly in love with you, I haven't a shred of dignity left, but neither of us is fit for marrying. I have my father at my back and you have your own demons."

"No" I said. I stopped his mouth with my hand, alarmed he might say more about the night in my cabin. Would I ever quell the memory of the madness and pain that overtook me when we tried to make love. The drink had taken its hold and now it was as clear as day to me that with the sacrament of a binding oath those phantoms of Black Hal that stood between me and Daniel would blow away for ever. I got to my feet and put my hands on my hips.

"As man and wife, all will be well."

Daniel shook his head. Everyone fell silent. I swayed on my feet and looked around at the men's faces. I could see they were indulging me in what they thought was a lovesick raving brought on by infatuation and too much wine. But nobody treated Queen Meg as a jest, my crew should know that very well by now. I was suddenly deadly serious.

"Cal, bring the carriage. We're going back to portside to find a ship with a captain who will marry us right away." No one moved. I felt cold-headed and very angry. "Will you do as I bid or do I have to saddle the horses myself?" I stared around the table. "You must all come with us. Luis, too. How would you like to see a real pirate wedding, sir? It will whet your appetite for your own, though yours will be a church affair, no doubt."

Still, no one moved. I drew my cutlass and pointed it at Flynn.

"Have you decided on mutiny, Quartermaster?"

"You're not thinking straight, mistress. Go to bed and sleep it off."

"What's wrong? Are you jealous because none of your harbour doxies want to marry you?"

"I've been married."

I swept the cutlass across the table, sending platters and cups clattering to the marble terrace.

"Marcelo! You would still be living in a stinking hovel if it wasn't for my bounty. Ready the carriage. I'm captain of this ship and we go to the harbour tonight."

I coughed and the sour taste of wine rose in my throat like bile. I felt myself come adrift as the black mood gripped me like a hungry animal. 'Hal's daughter,' someone whispered. I darted a look around but saw only dark silhouettes of trees, their branches stirring in the faint breeze. Daniel threw back his chair and tried to run inside the house. Flynn tackled him and they both rolled off the terrace. Marcelo leapt down after them. They dragged Daniel to his feet, all the men staggering and the worse for for drink. I stood over them, shouting.

"Tie him if you have to."

Daniel burst out laughing, an hysterical sound that echoed through the orchard.

"Don't bother with the ropes, I've worn them for many weeks now and I know when I'm beaten. She will have her way."

"You agree then?" I said.

"Of course not, it's vicious lunacy, but I'm done with fighting you. Have it how you please, though what end you expect from such a graceless beginning, I can't imagine."

"No, it will be well."

CHAPTER 29

I don't know who stepped in to keep the wedding party to a minimum rather than the procession I demanded. In the event, we comprised of Gower to guard Daniel and Flynn and Cal to act as witnesses. I remember little of getting into the carriage, except for Daniel hunched on the seat with his back turned to me and Marcelo taking the devil of a time to harness the horse. Cal climbed up and steered us away from the lamp lit house.

The warm night air sent the drink even more giddily to my head. We reached the deserted streets of the town and rumbled to a halt. I stumbled out of the carriage to lean against the still warm stones of an archway.

"Is there no damn captain to be had in this whole seaport?"

"Flynn's gone to find one." Gower put a reassuring hand on my arm. He stank of rum. "You should wait inside the carriage ma'am, out of sight."

I took a swig from the bottle I'd snatched from Marcelo's table. It burned my throat. I lurched over to the carriage and stared at Daniel who sat inside, pale as a statue.

"He won't talk to me." Pulling a face, I took another mouthful. The walls swayed around me as I staggered back. Cal joined Gower in trying to hold me still.

"Ma'am, get in the carriage. Your white dress stands out like a flag on the streets, even in the dark."

"I have to be married in white. Gower, where are my flowers?"

Gower opened the carriage door, leaned in and emerged with the tangled bunch of orchids and ferns I'd dragged from the pots outside Marcelo's house. I grabbed them from him and attempted to make a bouquet, scattering blooms on the pavement. Just then, we heard footsteps and Flynn appeared through the nearby archway with four unknown men following. They carried only one torch between them so it was hard to make out anyone's features.

"Captain Ned Carrington," Flynn. "Captain of the Silver Rose that stands offshore."

Carrington stood forward and took my hand. He would have had a pleasant face except for a long sword cut down the left cheek. He gave a low whistle.

"You're her, aren't you? Queen Meg herself."

"What's it to you?"

Carrington laughed. "Everything, if I'm to perform your wedding ceremony."

I suddenly remembered a piece of portside gossip. "Are you the Carrington who escaped gaol in Dublin?"

"What if I am? I'm not the only one here with a price on his head. Speaking of which, I'd like payment in full before we go to the ship."

"Half now, half after."

I nodded to Flynn who handed Carrington a purse of coin. Carrington shrugged then laughed again.

"I met Black Hal a couple of times. He boasted you were a beauty and for once he didn't lie. Let me round up my men and we'll set off to the ship right away. You'd better stow that carriage and horse, we'll walk from here. It's quicker and more discreet."

Gower opened the carriage door wide and hauled Daniel out. Carrington steered Gower and Daniel ahead to join his group of men. Daniel glanced back at me, his face unreadable.

"We'll have to tether the horse in the square here and hope it's safe for an hour or two," Flynn said.

I emptied the last of the rum down my throat and threw the bottle clattering against the wall.

"You'd better cover yourself with this, ma'am." Cal draped his coat around my shoulders and set his wide brimmed hat atop my ribboned hair.

I pulled the coat's coarse fabric under my chin and wrinkled my nose. "It smells of every port you've ever rolled around in."

It took me a moment to realise I was too drunk to walk unassisted. Cal grabbed hold of me before I keeled over. I cursed as the remnants of my bouquet scattered across the street. Flynn took my other arm and we set off after Ned's men. The streets seemed to wind forever.

"Are we to walk by way of Paraguay?" I complained. The walk was sobering me and I didn't welcome the sensation.

The men ahead of us disappeared through what seemed the hundredth archway. The torchlight wavered and dimmed as they drew ahead. I stumbled again. Flynn's breathing was loud in my ear as I leaned my weight on him. I'd forgotten he'd drunk his fair share too. We emerged into an empty square.

"Damn me, where are they?" Cal said.

He ran ahead to check each alley that led from the square. His silhouette bobbed in the dark shadows. Abruptly he stopped. I heard his feet clatter down a flight of stone steps directly ahead. Flynn and I hurried after him. From the top of the steps I could make out Cal's figure hunched below us and another shape, half in the shadows. He looked up, his face a pale smudge, his mouth agape.

"It's Gower! He's been attacked!"

Flynn sucked in a breath. "God's oath, they've kidnapped Daniel."

He left me swaying where I stood to race down the steps and hurl along the lanes in pursuit. I sat down heavily on the top step, shaking. Cal heaved Gower to sitting. I heard him groan. A black stain covered half his face. Cal's voice reached me clearly.

"It's a head wound. Your shawl, ma'am, I need to bind the cut."

Clumsily I dragged the shawl from around my neck and threw it, fluttering, down to Cal's outstretched hand. I heaved myself upright and started down the steps.

"Ma'am, where are you going?"

"I have to find Daniel."

"We can't do anything until Flynn sees where they're bound."

"It's obvious, Carrington's taken him to his stinking ship."

"We need to know for sure, and we need to get Gower to safety and attention for this wound. It's bad, ma'am. You'll have to bring the horse if you can."

The shock had almost sobered me completely. I could see the sense in Cal's words. With a brief wave to acknowledge him, I set off, hurrying back the way we had come. I was hard pressed to retrace my weaving steps along the maze of narrow streets. I began to weep. Pathetic, I know. Wasn't it my own folly that had led to Daniel being fair game for pirates, and that Gower should be hurt into the bargain?

I struggled on, opening my senses to catch any clues, the direction of the breeze, the murmur of far off waves. Suddenly, I recognised the entrance to the street where we had met Carrington. I thanked all the gods that the horse still stood in its harness, and the carriage was intact. I untied the beast and set off at an unsteady run back towards the steps. Cal met me halfway, supporting the weight of Gower's half-conscious body. Somehow we got him astride the horse and made our way to the carriage.

We manhandled Gower inside onto the seat that was strewn with the remains of my would-be wedding bouquet. The shawl around Gower's head was soaked dark with blood. I heard running footsteps and swung around, cutlass in hand. It was Flynn. He stopped and bent over to gather his breath.

"They've taken Daniel to the ship. Two of Ned's men were waiting for me a street away from where they ambushed Gower. They told me, at musket point, that Ned wants a high ransom. I should have seen it coming. He saw we were the worse for drink and took advantage of it."

I let out a curse. "Damn him to hell and back. I paid him well enough for the ceremony. When does he want this ransom?"

"By noon tomorrow, before tide turns and they set sail. I doubt they'll be as lenient as you. It will be pirate law and Daniel's head if you don't pay."

My breath stopped then rushed again through my chest. I forced my mind to sharpness.

"Cal, take Gower back to Marcelo's, have him attended to. Flynn, can you round up any of our men you can find who are staying around the port? There's an inn somewhere on this street I think? I remember passing it."

Flynn nodded.

"I'll wait for you there," I said. "Bring as many of the crew as you can muster. I won't lose Daniel to a cursed pirate like Ned Carrington."

I watched them both go then trudged back through the streets until I found the inn. By lucky chance, the landlord was from England. My Spanish is fair but I was relieved not to wrangle with language differences after the events of the night. I persuaded him to give me two rooms, a jug of water and a bowl of cold stew. I forced both down me in an effort to clear my head. All my thoughts turned on one thing, that they could have maimed or killed Daniel by now. I was sick at the thought of what I had done.

Whichever way you looked at it, I was no better than Carrington or any vicious pirate of the oceans. I had taken Daniel against his will and pressed him to my own ends. Love and passion were by the by. My actions were all greed and selfishness, and Daniel was paying the price for it.

CHAPTER 30

I don't think I knew how much I cared for Daniel until that day I feared for his life at the hands of pirate Ned Carrington. I waited in an upstairs room at the inn, keeping watch till daybreak, staring through dark timbered shutters that led to a shallow balcony. I was breathless with willing that Carrington would appear with his prisoner. It was as though I had woken from a stupor and glimpsed what I'd truly become.

Memories from the previous night were hazy, but there were enough glimpses that I regretted beyond words. If Carrington hadn't turned kidnapper I would have carried out my plan to marry Daniel, at sword point if necessary. When all was said and done I was no better than Hal, bullying my way around the world, taking what I wanted without heed for those I stole from.

I opened the shutters an inch further and gazed once more down the street. Red roofs and white painted houses were splashed with dusty green palm trees. In the distance the ocean shone a glinting ribbon of pale blue. My head throbbed in the sunlight. I got up from the window and retreated into the cool room to force another cup of water down my throat. The landlord had brought a tray after I paid him for the two rooms but the boiled eggs and warm bread set my stomach churning. I had never willingly drunk so much in my life and I swore it would be the last. Dutch courage, they call it when you use drink to force yourself past the restraint of natural inhibitions. Well, I had seen the grasping creature that lay beyond my tenth cup of wine and I never wished to meet her again.

My so called wedding dress lay crumpled on the floor where I had tossed it. I was in man's garb now, another purchase from the landlord. The velveteen jacket, pants, tall boots and grey cape would be my costume for a long time to come. Now my only thought and purpose rested on Daniel. He must be safe. After that, the rest mattered very little.

The sound of voices from below had me leaping to the door. There was a creak on the stairs then Flynn opened my door without knocking. He ushered in Joshua, and Hugh Catter.

"Carrington's on his way," he said. "I sent the message out that we would pay their terms. John Blaine's been spying their ship for us. He saw five men drop a boat and row ashore."

Catter must have seen how anxious I was. Unbidden, he put a hand on my arm to reassure me. I flinched then softened my response with an awkward smile.

"You're all good men who've followed me through thick and thin. I'm relying on you again today. We have to get Daniel back. Carrington must not harm him. It's my fault, I've wrecked a good young man's life."

"All will be well, mistress," Joshua said. The fear in his eyes belied his words. "We have four of our men rounded up and waiting close by, should there be need."

Flynn, who was standing at the window, raised a hand. "They're here." He leaned out then stepped onto the balcony so he could be seen from the street. I saw him wave and give one low whistle before he turned back into the room, closing the shutters behind him.

"It's Ned and four others."

"Daniel's with them?"

He nodded.

"Bundled under a cloak, a man on either side."

I took a shuddering breath. Footsteps thumped on the stairs. I heard the landlord say a word then Carrington's men were at the door. Joshua flung it open before they knocked. Ned walked in followed by two others. He looked very pleased with himself. I spoke first to take the advantage.

"You injured one of my men and took another prisoner."

Carrington was having none of my bravado. "I'd have taken you too if your men hadn't stayed so damned close. Did you bring the ransom?"

"It's being fetched,"

His face darkened. "You don't intend to cheat me, I hope."

"Show me the prisoner."

"He's safe enough in the next room."

"I want to see him."

"When I've seen the colour of your money."

I strode past him and was out the door before anyone could stop me. Ned's men caught me on the landing as I dragged open the door to the adjoining room. A scuffle broke out as Joshua and Catter wrestled the men off me. I barely noticed. My entire focus was on the figure of Daniel, slumped on the bed, hands bound and a sack covering his head. My heart wrenched at the indignity, at the memory of having done the same to him myself. A surly looking pirate sat next to Daniel, gripping his arm.

Carrington and one of his men dragged me back to my room. I kicked and pulled at them until Flynn intervened, pushing the men off me. "Stop this! The landlord will have the militia here if you don't keep it down."

Inside my room, I slumped in a chair. Joshua tried to give me a cup of water but I waved him off. I was shocked, but not by the undignified scuffle. I replayed what I had just seen of

Daniel as he was held prisoner in the room next door. In the brief glimpse I had of him, it was plain as day that the prisoner wasn't Daniel. He wore Daniel's clothes and was of like build and height, but the hands gave him away. I'd know Daniel's fine fingers and the colour of his skin anywhere. God knows, I'd studied him enough.

I got my face in order before standing up to confront Carrington. He stood, cocksure, in the middle of the rug but I saw the momentary flicker of anxiety in his eyes. It was enough to confirm what my instincts told me. The prisoner wasn't Daniel and Ned Carrington was bent on tricking us. I fought to keep my own expression impassive.

"Very well. He seems unharmed. You'll have your ransom. My man's on his way with it and should be here within a half hour. Or you can settle for a quarter payment that I have here in my purse."

I jangled the coin pouch that hung at my belt. Carrington didn't respond but I knew he was weighing it up, a quick getaway or hold out for a bigger prize. I walked to the table and poured wine into half a dozen cups.

"You're welcome to eat." I was surprised at how steady my voice and hands were.

"Catter, Flynn, take a drink, won't you?"

Catter looked surprised. It was a rare thing to be waited on by Queen Meg, but Flynn had read something in my expression. He held out a hand then at a faint nod from me he dropped the cup clumsily and I let the jug follow after. I stooped with him as wine spilled out across the wooden floor.

As our heads met, I spoke quietly and clearly in his ear. "It's not Daniel. He must still be on Ned's ship."

Flynn stood up, making a business of wiping my hand with a napkin and retrieving the empty jug. "I'll see to it, milady."

He turned and left the room while I walked back to the table and handed out plates of bread and sliced cheese to Carrington and his men. They accepted greedily, seeing nothing amiss in Queen Meg serving them. In any case my casual manner and the unexpected food distracted them. It was well past the half hour before Carrington began to grumble again.

"Five more minutes and we take him back to the ship. Or maybe we'll just throw him in the harbour on our way."

I frowned. "I've more cause to worry than you. That's my gold being walked about the streets. Joshua, go down and ask the landlord if anyone has arrived."

Carrington put up a hand. "Stay where you are. I don't like the smell of this. Where's your other man gone to anyway?"

"Probably set out to meet John Blaine who's bringing the gold. I told him to keep an eye on the business." I untied the purse from my belt and held it out. "Won't you take this in good faith? There's more than quarter of it here."

Carrington snatched the purse, weighed it in his palm then pulled the strings to look inside. He prodded a skinny forefinger among the coins. "Throw in those earrings and I'll think about it."

I touched a hand to my ear. "They're sapphires," I said, though they were nothing of the kind. "Precious stones, and a sentimental gift."

Carrington reached forward and unhooked one, none too gently, from my ear. Out the corner of my eye I saw Catter readying himself to jump between us.

"It's all right Hugh, it's a fair trade." I never took my eyes from Ned. Unhooking the other sapphire, I held it up to the light. "Set in fine silver, a diamond droplet on each."

Carrington's greed won out. He snatched the earring from me.

"I'll take the jewels, the coin and a couple of your rings to seal the bargain."

"It's a very hard bargain, Ned."

"I'm a pirate," Carrington smirked. "You know how it is."

He held out a calloused palm to shake on the deal. I let go reluctantly, suddenly afraid that Flynn had not had enough time to get to Carrington's ship. In the next moment Carrington was leaving the room. His men followed, the last of them stuffing the remaining cheese in his pocket. They hurried downstairs as I leaned over the stairwell to watch them go. The landlord appeared in the downstairs lobby as they ran past.

"Everything all right, ma'am?"

"Yes. We'll all be gone by midday and leave you in peace."

He nodded and disappeared. I stayed for a moment, leaning over the stair rail. Suddenly I realised that the pirate who guarded the unknown 'prisoner' hadn't left with Carrington and the others. Most likely they had stayed back to rob me when my gold arrived. Carrington was greedy enough to risk it. I looked around to see Catter standing behind me. I beckoned him to listen with me at the door of the next room. He caught my meaning at once and, finger to lips, waved for Joshua to leave my room and join us.

There was a moment of deathly quiet then, at a nod from me, Joshua kicked the door open. He leapt back just in time to avoid the musket shot that blasted out. Catter grabbed a stool and threw it inside the room. The ruse worked. Another shot fired then Joshua and Catter rushed in before Carrington's men had a chance to recover. 'Daniel,' now minus the hood, was trying to reload the musket that had fired the second shot. My men disarmed him and the other pirate and had them tied up, gagged and the door closed on them again before the landlord came rushing up the stairs. I ran down to intercept him.

"We caught an armed thief. He tagged on to our visitors but all is well. We'll take him to the militia and sorry for the disturbance."

"You're not harmed?"

"Quite safe. Thanks for your concern, and your patience. My men will see to everything."

I retired to my own chamber, having no wish to look at the man who had impersonated Daniel and wore his clothes. I was anxious enough that Carrington may have killed Daniel already. I prayed Flynn would arrive in time and swore to all the gods that I would pay any price to ensure Daniel would never risk harm again. In a heartbeat, I knew what I had to do.

Bending over, I pulled off my boot to retrieve a leather pouch that held the last of my coins. I checked the contents to make sure it would suffice. Opening the door, I called softly to the next room. "Joshua." He appeared at once. "Are Carrington's men secure?"

"Catter has them tied up like turkeys at Christmas time."

"I need you to do something for me, urgent and confidential." I pressed the bag of money into his hand. "Take this and buy two berths on the next merchant ship sailing to England."

"Beg pardon ma'am, but if they get Daniel from the ship you won't need to run, will you? Ned will have to sail on the next tide if he wants to make a break for it, and that's at three o'clock."

"Just do it."

He bowed and hurried off, bumping into Catter who had apparently been downstairs to talk to the landlord. Catter gave Joshua a curious look then nodded to me.

"We have the landlord's assurance he won't cause problems as long as we have the criminals out within the hour. I think he's taken a fancy to you, ma'am," he said with a grin.

I couldn't raise a smile back. He ushered me inside my room and poured us each a cup of wine. He saw how anxious I was and kept a tactful silence. He went out a couple of times to check the prisoners were still secure. I left the wine untouched and stood to wait at the window for what seemed an eternity.

It was almost an hour later when, by every miracle, I saw a group of men walking down the street towards the inn. I ran out on the balcony to lean out. There was Flynn, Jack Lance and four other seamen. It took only a heartbeat to see that one of the roughly dressed buccaneers was Daniel. He was the first to look up at me. It was a moment that felt more precious than the whole patchwork of my chaotic life put together. I took a deep and shuddering sigh. Daniel lived and was safe.

CHAPTER 31

I stood at the top of the stairs, holding my breath until I could see him. My mouth tasted salt and I realised tears were streaming down my face. I hastily wiped them away with the back of my hand and shook my head to compose myself. It wouldn't do for Queen Meg to be snivelling, though I wanted to cry and scream 'He's alive!' at the top of my lungs.

"Ma'am!'

I looked down to see the landlord standing in the hall at the bottom of the stairs.

"More men at the door for you." I could see he'd had enough. "I can't let them in until you get rid of the ruffian who was shooting on my premises."

"Apologies, I'm sorry to test your patience. We knocked the man out in the skirmish and he's just coming to. And I'm afraid he had an accomplice with him who we managed to flush out. If you would, please tell the man called Jack Lance to bring two others to escort the burglars to the militia."

Breathing heavily, the landlord stamped off. A moment later, Jack sprinted upstairs with two of our new recruits. Carrington's men were still bound and gagged so they caused little trouble. They were soon hauled out of the room next to mine and bundled downstairs. I caught Jack's arm as he went past and drew him to one side.

"You can't take them to the militia or they'll inform on us. Take them portside so they are within running distance of Carrington's ship. If you hurry they'll catch it before the tide turns and we'll be rid of them."

I followed the men downstairs, my thoughts turning to Daniel again. What could I say after I'd put him in mortal danger? After the drunken wedding charade? My tongue was heavy as a stone and my heart banged in my chest.

The landlord appeared and nodded to me politely enough, though I saw his patience was stretched to the limit. We stood together and watched as Carrington's men were led off.

"You disturbed the peace of my inn, if you don't mind me saying so. Your other visitors are in the courtyard. You'll oblige me by not taking long about your business."

He nodded curtly and left me in the hall. I walked to the rear of the tavern as if in a dream. A dim passage gave way to a courtyard. The sunbaked wall was stacked with barrels and overhung by bougainvillea. Daniel stood there, Flynn at his side. I couldn't meet Daniel's gaze.

"Thank you, Flynn. You got him out alive."

"It was Jack that managed it. He climbed on board, bold as brass, and managed to run below without anyone seeing him. Daniel was in the first cabin below deck and only one man guarding him. Captain Ned must have been very sure of himself."

"Did they hurt him, Daniel I mean?" I said. I addressed Flynn, though Daniel was standing right in front of me.

"Hit him around a bit, trying to find out what he knew about your plans. Gave you a couple of sore ribs I think, Master Stede?'

"I didn't tell them anything." The sound of Daniel's voice made me look at him at last.

"I don't see why you should have protected me when all I've done is put your life in danger." The words ran from my mouth before I could stop them.

"I wouldn't give him the satisfaction. Besides, you have some good men in your crew. I shouldn't like to hand them over to such a villain as Ned Carrington."

Flynn clapped Daniel on the shoulder and laughed. "You have grit, I'll give you that. Though, even with those clothes, you'd hardly make a pirate."

Daniel grinned back at him. To my fevered gaze, the sun blazed brighter. I had rarely seen Daniel smile, indeed why would he, held against his will and dragged half way around the world.

Joshua suddenly appeared, and did a double take at Daniel's appearance. "Good work Flynn, you sprung the prisoner!" He dug a hand in the front of his tunic, drew out a folded parchment and handed it to me. "Two berths as you requested, ma'am. You need to hurry. She's a merchant galleon called the Nottingham and she sails to England on the afternoon tide. You'll be passing Ned in the harbour."

I nodded thanks and stood for a long moment, fingering the parchment. Somewhere a bell began to chime the midday. I held out the parchment to Daniel.

"Mister Stede, this is your freedom. You're no longer my prisoner. Flynn will take the second berth and escort you safe and sound back to your father." I turned to Flynn before he could protest. "I'm sorry, Flynn. I don't want to lose you but there's no one else I would trust so well with the job."

I turned to leave so I didn't have to look at the delighted relief I would see in Daniel's face. His next words stopped me in my tracks.

"You could come with me."

"I'm a pirate," I said, my back to him. "Like Ned Carrington, like the General who I slaughtered."

I felt a hand on my arm. Daniel turned me to face him.

"I heard what happened to you. You were kidnapped when you were just a girl. Meg, you weren't raised to this and you don't have to be what he made you, Black Hal or whatever he calls himself."

I was stunned to the core that they, my men, spoke of it behind my back. I pulled my arm from his grasp. A wave of hot shame washed through me.

"How dare you pity me! So, the men pick over my past, make up stories about it, do they? Think about your own plight, Daniel Stede. Run home while you have the chance to do it. Queen Meg has given you reprieve."

Daniel gripped my shoulders to stop me from flinging away from him. I wanted to cut him down.

"Your men love you, Meg. They would follow you to hell and back. They know how you care for them, they talk of your loyalty and bravery. Those are the stories they tell, how you gave a life to this man or that when he had nowhere else to turn."

It was as though the courtyard and the blue sky above were ripping apart at Daniel's words. I was shocked to the core that my men spoke of me with admiration, not because I was invincible Queen Meg. And this fine young man cared for me, I saw it in his eyes. I was shaking. Panic ran through me like a fever.

"Get him out of here!"

I wrenched myself free of Daniel's hands and raced out of the courtyard to the refuge of the inn. My hands clutched at my coat, at each other, trying to hold her together in one piece, Queen Meg, the woman I had made myself become. She was the Queen who ensured I survived Black Hal. I couldn't let her fall, not ever. Even for Daniel Stede.

CHAPTER 32

Flynn and Daniel caught the merchant ship before it sailed, or so Catter told me a couple of hours later. I paid our bill at the inn, the landlord friendly again now he was rid of his troublesome guests. We stayed at Marcelo's villa for another week. Gower refused a doctor so Joshua, who had some rudimentary medical knowledge, tended him as best he could. Catter took regular rides into the port to pick up any tidbits of news. As for me, I was sunk in a gloom so deep I could barely stir from the house to take a walk or a ride. I couldn't remember such dark depression, not even when I had first lost my home.

One Sunday morning, Marcelo and Luis persuaded Cal, who hated walking, to stroll to church with them. Luis tried to recruit me in their outing.

"It's a beautiful view over the hill." He gestured beyond the garden and orchard trees. "On a sunny day like this, it would be good for the soul, like a pilgrimage."

"I haven't been inside a church since I was a girl, Luis, and I'm in no mood for it now. I plan to sit on the terrace, gaze at the sun and drink coffee as black as I can stand it."

After they left, I took a book to read along with my coffee, but as usual these days, I barely got past one page. Not a day went by that I didn't think of Flynn. He had been beside me since the day I escaped Black Hal. As for Daniel, I obsessed about him hour by crawling hour, bereft that I'd let him go, that my lunatic dream of us wedded would never be. I was rudderless, cast adrift from past or future. I felt trapped in a nether-world that was bounded by the white villa and the distant purple hills. I let the melancholy take me under and waited, with some defiance, for a hand or rope that would pull me to the surface again.

Around mid-morning Pedlar brought me more coffee, a dish of sweet oranges and a decanter of wine. He also carried a box under one arm. He opened it and drew out a chequered board and a set of chess pieces.

"Beg your pardon, ma'am, but it would do you good to get in a fighting mood again. Would you care to take me on?"

He looked rested and well fed, his face flushed with the sun.

"You seem content here. Perhaps the farmer's life would do you better than on board ship."

"Perhaps. Though the sea and chilly old England still pull at me."

He swung the board around so that the white rows of chess figures were ranged in front of me. I picked up the queen. The marble piece was exquisitely carved and weighed heavy in my hand. I shifted the board so that I played the black.

"You first."

I beat Pedlar so easily that I wondered if he was letting me win. Suddenly, I remembered that I was good at this. My father had taught me, regularly and with a seriousness that had fixed the patterns of play firmly in my mind and I could give him a run for his money. In any case Pedlar seemed happy enough to be beaten. He set up the pieces for another game. Gower and Joshua wandered on to the terrace to watch us and enjoy the warm air. I nodded at Gower.

"You seem better."

He rubbed his cheek and touched the bandage that still covered his head wound.

"I think Ned's men may have knocked some sense into me. I'm thinking of giving up the pirate ways and settling here for a while."

His remark took me by surprise. I didn't like the feeling that welled up in my throat. Another parting, another loss.

"You won't take one more jaunt with us on the Night Wing?"

"No, ma'am, if you'll let me go. I'm close to forty and this knock on the head has made me think I won't live forever. I always had the notion I'd set up with a family of my own, if I could find a woman who doesn't look too carefully at my past. I like this place. I think it might be as good as any to put down roots."

Joshua chimed in. "Marcelo said he could stay here until he finds his own place."

So, they'd been discussing it out of my earshot. I made light of it to cover my dismay.

"You're all to leave me then and become farmers and gauchos."

"Not all, ma'am," Gower said. "Just me."

I made an effort to throw off the melancholy that hung around me. "A toast!" I poured measures of wine and passed them round. "To Gower making a grand new life!"

"And to the Night Wing," Joshua said. "Cal told me she's fit and ready to sail whenever you are."

"The Night Wing."

As I swallowed down the sweet thick wine I realised I had been holding out for news of Daniel, yearning to know if he was safe and home. That waiting had stranded me. I knew full well it could be weeks before he touched English shores. I made a decision.

"It's time we sailed." I put down my glass. "How about the day after tomorrow, boys? We'll take some of my treasure to fit us out with provisions, then the world's our oyster."

The men halloo-ed but my heart was heavy as ship's timber.

In the end we didn't stay to pull my treasure from the cave where I'd stowed it. The morning before we set sail, Cal told me of a pirate galleon that had been spotted just twenty miles off, sailing east at speed and with a full cargo. So began the next chapter of adventures for the Night Wing and Queen Meg. We took the booty and the galleon too then sailed east with the trade winds until we came across another fair and fat vessel ripe for the picking. We ran hard at the ship, taking it easily. It was an ill-kept bucket that turned out to belong to Robert 'Cutthroat' Shaw, an old and ailing buccaneer who should have given up the sea years ago. I addressed him as he stood, hands bound, on my deck.

"What shall we do with you, Master Robert?"

He looked murderous, as well he might. His crew had surrendered at the first sally and we had his ship, the Golden Necklace, added to our growing flotilla. Shaw squinted at me like an old seabird.

"I'll serve you, Queen Meg."

"You always were a terrible liar."

He spat and shifted pathetically in the worn boots I remembered from at least four years before. Some of my men laughed but I took pity on him.

"Here's the bargain for you, take it or leave it. I'll keep your ship and whoever of your men swear solemn oath to Queen Meg. My bosun tells me you have a good quantity of coin and jewels on board. You can keep one third of it but I'm putting you ashore at the next port. "

Cutthroat knew he'd made a lucky escape. He even shook my hand when we put him in a rowboat at the Antilles.

We didn't linger but set sail east in a fair wind and swift current. That night the crew threw a party on deck, carousing till dawn. I retired early to pore over maps and call up dreams of wind and weather. I couldn't follow Daniel but I could still be Meg, Queen of the seven seas and all besides.

In the weeks that followed the Night Wing picked off one buccaneer and merchant ship after the other. We gained a small armada of six vessels, all with cargo holds bulging treasure. I don't know why our luck held so long to bring us such easy spoils but the sea raids were a welcome distraction. The days and hours between saw me lying on my bed or pacing my cabin floor, gripped by a melancholy so black I could think of nothing think to appease it.

As the days wore on, I realised my sadness wasn't only for the loss of Daniel. His departure had left a deeper wound that wouldn't heal. I never knew how much I mourned my old life, the life before Hal, until Daniel had brought the echo of it back into my world. And I was still shocked at how deep Hal had hurt me until that night in my cabin with Daniel, when the terrifying pain of my past had stopped me joining with him.

CHAPTER 33

The sea raids became my purpose. We took longer and longer routes to pursue every rumour of a pirate ship. King Chevas, John of Manse, Red Jack, Irish Pat, they all fell under the Night Wing's attacks. Still it didn't fill Queen Meg's belly or the ache in her heart.

One evening, I went to Jack Lance's cramped cabin, the one that used to be Flynn's, and asked him to look through the maps with me one more time. Cal joined us, bringing cups of ale. I could see neither of them had their hearts in the task. The weather was sultry, the parchments damp and curling at the edges. Cal stuck his dagger in one corner of the topmost chart to keep it flat. Jack was uncharacteristically ill tempered.

"We've traversed these seas back and forth until the men are dizzy," he said. "The only route left is north east if we are to find fresh waters and a port to rest in."

"Be careful," I said. "You're not Quartermaster yet, even if you'd like to be."

Cal chimed in. "Can we not cut some of these vessels loose, sell them in Spain, take a few weeks ashore?" He barely kept the edge of irritation out of his voice. Sweat glistened on his face. "You've been generous with the booty. The men are itching to take a break and spend some of it. Sickness is creeping on board. Jack's right, we need fresh food and water."

"Am I running a pirate ship or a foundling home for babies?"

I thrust the charts off the table. The one with Cal's dagger in it ripped across. I stormed out and ran up on deck. The men had spoken the truth and I felt it like a hard knot in my gut. I was as exhausted as they were but afraid to stop or go ashore, terrified to stop moving in case the melancholy took me over altogether. A couple of the men looked at me curiously as I gripped the ship's side and took a deep lung full of the fetid air. The tantrum, born of fear, left me. The men didn't deserve to be driven on like galley slaves. Besides, the last thing I wanted was a mutiny. I hurtled back down the ladder, almost colliding with Jack at the bottom of it.

"You've had your say, and you make a good point. Set course for due north east and Spain. Five days should see us there. Tell the men extra rations all round."

I hurried to my cabin before he could reply. I hadn't done it as graciously as I might, but I had conceded.

We made Cadiz in six days of plain sailing and I slept for most of them. Cal went ashore as soon as we weighed anchor, primed to fix arrangements with the excise men. I sent Joshua off with the first row boat of men keen to be ashore. He liked nothing better than to drive a hard bargain so I gave him free rein to sell the extra vessels we'd picked up on our raids. I stood on deck as he climbed over the side and grasped the rope to let down to the boat, already half full of buccaneers.

"I'll keep the Sea Folly," I said. "With a refit of the main mast she'll keep speed with the Night Wing and make a useful decoy."

Joshua nodded and dropped down hand over hand to the bobbing row boat. A light drizzle spattered the air and I looked up to let it cool my cheeks. The weather was still humid and the dockside air less than fresh. I was suddenly aware of not having changed clothes for a week. The men's pantaloons I wore itched like the devil. Still I waited until Cal returned with sure news of our safe entry. He was in the return boat, waving and smiling at me as he pulled alongside. I gripped his hand as he scrambled on board.

"You've changed your complaining tune," I said.

He grinned. "The excise on duty is Jorges, same as last time. I squared it easy. It helps that I speak Spanish like a Castilian and that he's still a corrupt son of a whore."

I nodded approval.

"Good work. You can go ashore with the next boat if you like. I'm staying here for now,"

I went below to my cabin as the next boat load of seamen lined up to take their overdue shore leave. The ship needed a good clean up, that was for certain, but the state of my cabin was my own affair. I had never neglected it so badly before. I felt queasy when I saw the mess of food remnants, linen and books strewn everywhere, slops still in the pot by the bed. I'd turned into a slattern.

Was I such a hopeless fool that my disappointment with Daniel, my sick rage over Hal, had led me to this? My behaviour smacked of a self loathing that I couldn't afford to indulge. Nonetheless, cleaning the cabin was beyond my capacity for the moment. It would have to be stripped and fumigated along with the rest of the ship. For now I conceded defeat, packed a few books and clothes in a bag and heaved it up the ladder to take on the next boat ashore.

Cadiz was busier than I remembered even three years ago. It was still full of Genovese and more Irish merchants than ever. The lodgings Cal found for us were in one of the smaller merchant houses topped by a tower like the scores of others that overlooked the harbour. My room and bed were small but comfortable enough and I settled into a desultory routine of sleeping long and late. After dark, I had one or two of the men accompany me on long rides and walks, and even the occasional swim at Caluna.

By the end of the week Joshua had sold two of the spare ships outright and was bargaining a third. At dusk that same day Cal came to tell me the Night Wing had been cleaned and minor repairs finished. He found me at the stables across the street from our lodgings where I had a horse saddled and ready for my evening ride.

"Do you want to inspect the ship?" he said.

I stroked the mare's glossy black flank with my gloved hand.

"No. If I step on board I'll want to sail again right away." I glanced at Cal, his dark aquiline features etched in the lamplight. "Is it only me who longs so for the sea?"

Cal shrugged. "I've felt ship's timbers under my feet since I was sixteen, ma'am. There's no greater adventure, but I confess I need this change. I couldn't believe how our luck held on those raids and I began to feel we were courting disaster more than once."

"I never knew you were afraid," I said. But then I'd only been bent on racing us from one conquest to the next with no thought of danger.

"I'm often afraid, ma'am." His teeth gleamed in the shadows. "It's the reason I'm still alive."

There was a sudden commotion across the street. It was coming from an archway that linked the corners of two of the houses. A figure broke from the shadows and ran across to us.

"Milady!"

It was Pedlar. He looked shocked out of his wits.

"There's a sailor." He gestured towards the huddle of three dark figures opposite. "He says he has a message for you – from Flynn."

"Flynn! News at last, thank God."

I took off immediately, Pedlar racing after. "Wait!" he said. "It's not what you think."

The group of men turned out to be Catter with a new recruited seaman called Tam Burnett. With them was a young man I'd never seen before. He looked barely sixteen but with a swagger on him that belied his years.

"Are you her? Queen Meg?"

I chose to ignore his bad manners. "You have a message from Flynn?"

"I won't tell you of it here."

I didn't want to take them up to my room so I led Jem across the street to where Pedlar was tying up the horse. Tam ran off, his errand accomplished. Unhooking the single lantern from the post I opened the door to a store room behind the stall. We all crowded inside. I held up the lantern to look at the young man's features. He had the face of a farm boy, newly recruited to the sea. His innocent gaze and fair complexion was belied with something crafty about his mouth.

"Who are you and what's your ship?"

"Jem Davies of the Tamarind. It's a merchant galleon."

"Then tell your story, Jem Davies, and come quickly to the point."

"We put in at Casablanca eight days ago, planning to sail here the next day to unload the cargo. A man told me I'd be paid well if I took a message straight to Queen Meg. He said to tell you that Flynn gives you this."

He dug in his pocket and held out a ring on his flat palm. The ring was ornately wrought jade. It was Flynn's all right, from his mother. He was never without it, if not on his hand then strung on a chain around his neck. 'When I find a girl as good as my mother she shall have it,' he used to joke. My chest gripped with dread.

"Who was the man who gave you this?"

"He wouldn't tell me except he was with the Hell's Mouth, captained by Black Hal."

My vision swam. I drew out my dagger and flashed it in front of Jem's face. Catter grabbed him by the arm. His fist was bunched and ready should Jem try to attack me. Jem's expression turned surly.

"No need for that," he said. "The buccaneer paid me to tell you, and bring the ring to your very hand."

"Tell me what?"

It was worse than imaginable. Flynn was in Black Hal's clutches.

"You must go to Casablanca port. Hal's on business but will return there in one week."

Jem held out the ring and dropped it in my hand. My fingers closed on it, tight.

"What does the blackguard want?"

"He wants Queen Meg to go back to him, in exchange for Flynn's life."

Time seemed to flicker and stand still.

Pedlar coughed and spat on the ground behind him.

"What do you want us to do with him, ma'am?"

"Nothing, except get him out of my sight."

Jem didn't need any prompting. He shouldered past us and out the storeroom door. He turned and pointed at me.

"You're to meet Hal at El Circa boarding house. It's on the portside." With that, he disappeared into the night.

Pedlar broke the stunned silence. "Do you trust him?"

I held up the ring. It shone dully in the lamplight. "I trust this. Flynn would have never given it willingly. I have no choice. We sail on the next tide."

"The next tide is at six in the morning," Catter said.

"Then we must act now. Round up as many of the crew as you can muster. And find me Jack Lance. I need his expertise to plot a route south and get to Casablanca before Hal returns."

"Jack's gone inland. He and a half dozen of the others rode out to explore for a few days."

My heart sank. "Then we'll manage without him." I shoved past Catter into the courtyard. He hurried after and stood to face me.

"You can't sail to meet Black Hal with only half your men. This message has 'trap' written all over it."

"Do you think I don't know that? It's unthinkable but here it is, somehow, somewhere, Hal has Flynn. I have to go. I'll see you all on board before first light."

CHAPTER 34

Without another word, Catter, Pedlar and Cal went off to make ready. The lantern swung in my right hand, Flynn's ring was clutched in my left. I extinguished the light and turned my face to the stars, opening my senses to the night, the smell of the ocean and the drift of a breeze from the sea. I smelt it – by tomorrow a strong wind would blow in from the west. If we could race ahead of it we could reach Casablanca in six days, even less.

It was like a knife to my heart that I should have to set eyes on Hal, much less parlay with him. But I couldn't see a way out of it, not while there was a chance Flynn was still alive. And, while I would risk all to ensure Flynn's safety, I was also afraid for Daniel. I had to know if he was safe home in Cornwall. There had been plenty of time for Flynn to take him there and make his way back to the Moroccan coast, but who knew if Hal had captured them both when they disembarked in Plymouth?

There was no point in speculating every black possibility so I set my mind to working on a plan. The idea came immediately. If we were in Casablanca's waters ahead of Hal, ready for him as he neared the coast, we would have time to set up the Sea Folly as a decoy. I would pack her with every buccaneer she could hold, hidden and armed to the teeth. For myself, I would be one of a handful of crew standing at the prow. We would load enough booty on deck to fool Hal into thinking we were using her as a cargo ship. The Night Wing would sail a few miles behind, well out of Hal's reach. The Sea Folly would sail close enough to be in earshot so Hal could bargain with me over Flynn. Close enough and my men would break out of hiding and swarm the Hell's Mouth before Hal knew the danger.

Over and over, I played the scene in my mind. Presuming Flynn was on board, we would rescue him and scupper the Hell's Mouth to the bottom of the ocean. As I thought of Hal escaping the explosives we had set for him in Torsand, my anger grew. The man surely had nine lives and a pact with the devil. One thing I was sure of - if and when we had Flynn safe and sound there would be such a reckoning that Harry would curse the day he kidnapped my best and most loyal sailor.

I hurried back inside the tavern to collect my belongings and leave a bag of coin for the landlord to find when he woke. The last thing I wanted was for the excise to come running after us for bad debts.

Our exit from Cadiz harbour was quick and smooth. I settled down impatiently, and uncomfortably, for the voyage. All but eight of my men were crammed on the Sea Folly with barely an inch to swing a cat. I made myself visible on deck. Joshua and Pedlar navigated the Night Wing a few furlongs behind. Cal acted as captain and Quartermaster of the Sea Folly while Catter did his best with the sea charts to keep us on course.

On the afternoon of the sixth day, with the west wind howling behind us, we made the coast of Casablanca and tucked the ships closer in to shore. The current rolled as we tacked a course through it, trying to avoid the unfamiliar breakers. But our luck held. Before an hour went by the boy on the crow's nest yelled out.

"Sail!"

My neck prickled. I knew it was him, it was Hal and the Hell's Mouth. I rushed to portside and peered through the telescope. There she was, framed in the perfect circle of the glass. Even in the grey sheeting rain that began to pour, her black sails and fluttering pennant were unmistakable. I shouted over the wind to Catter who joined me at the rail.

"The dog tried to get here before us. Take over the wheel and steer hard forward."

I checked that all the men on the Sea Folly except a handful were stowed out of sight below. I made the signal to Jed to haul the white flag.

The pennant went up, swift as a bird. We sailed on towards Hal's ship. Every moment, we braced for a warning shot or sally from the Hell's Mouth but nothing came. It seemed my ruse of presenting on board the Sea Folly had worked. Hal was letting us near. The rain and wind were on our side. We would have to draw alongside if we were to communicate at all. Still, I watched like a hawk. I didn't put it past the old sea dog to turn about and try to duck our bows before we were in range. We drew closer.

I scanned the decks of Hell's Mouth for any sign of Hal. There was none, or indeed of any crew at all. Judging by his exclamation, Catter realised the same moment I did. As the worst of the rainstorm drifted away, we could see that the black sails of Hal's ship were rigged wrong. She sat too low in the water and with cracks and gunshot holes peppering her side.

This bucket wasn't Hell's Mouth, it was a derelict galleon dressed up to look like Hal's ship. The devil had out-tricked me. The next second proved how far he had turned the tables on my attempt to thwart him at Torsand. A rowboat skimmed off from the galleon's side. Hanging, almost to the water, was a single rope, soaked in pitch.

As if in slow motion the rowboat's oarsman stood up and lit the rope. He and the other man in the boat plied hard, racing to reach a safe distance before the fire reached the galleon's deck. As for us, we had no hope of turning the Sea Folly in time to escape. I watched in horror as the flame raced along the rope. The blast caught us full in the bow. Whipped by the raging wind, the heavens seemed to hail burnings masts and sails. A surge of water smacked into the Sea Folly's side and we were over, keeled almost upside down, crashing into the burning remnants of the galleon.

Those of us above went overboard first, plunged into the ocean from the flailing deck that sat perpendicular as a smooth, water-racked wall. I was catapulted from the ship's side to smash into a broken mast. I tried to grasp and cling to the tattered edge of a sail but the ship heaved like a whale and I dropped into the ocean. Water poured in my ears and mouth as I struggled to right myself. In the terrifying, churning waves, the bottom of the Sea Folly stood like black ragged battlements before me.

In that split second I thought of the scores of men trapped below by the pounding water. The laden Sea Folly sank like a stone. Then all my mind was consumed by panic. I flailed in the inky water. Somehow, I loosed my sword belt and cloak and scaped off my boots, toe by toe. The release of weight buoyed me up like a cork. Lungs burning, I struck up to the surface.

A black shape floated above me and I grabbed it. It was a broken spar. With all my strength I heaved my head and shoulders above the water's surface. I sucked in air before another wave beat down, plunging me under once more. I held on to that piece of timber for dear life. After an endless, churning minute it bobbed me to the surface again. Ash and remnants of burnt sails blew in the sky like carrion birds. I fought to hold on through the next rolling bank of water. I was so disoriented I could only hope the drag and suck of the waves were pummelling me towards the shore.

Suddenly I was being lifted, not by the waves but by a pair of hands. Dazed, I felt the bite of a rope as it was passed under my arms. Someone yelled out.

"Keep fast and row like the devil!"

The water surged under me but this time I was dragged above it and landed like a fish on the deck of a wide bottomed row boat. My ears roared and I vomited water. More hands pulled me to sitting and poured a scalding mouthful of rum down my throat. I caught a spinning glimpse of sky ribboned by dark clouds. I wretched again and blacked out.

CHAPTER 35

I woke to find myself dressed in fresh dry clothes and lying on a sofa that was draped in velvet. A sharp recollection of drowning pulled me to sitting but the swaying room had me lie down again. My throat and eyes were sore. I looked around. The room I was in had high ceilings, ornate chairs, an enormous woven rug and vases crammed with thick scented orchids. A heavy damask curtain covered the long window. With a shock, I recognised where I was - the El Circa boarding house in Casablanca. You would have to be Blind Pirate Jack not to know the trade here was flesh.

I remembered it from my last visit to Casablanca. From the street it looked like a palace but it was a whore's den inside. On that occasion three of my men had fetched up here after a hard night's drinking. They were in search of a slattern apiece and sampled the goods without being able to pay the bill. For that, they ran foul of the Mmdame, Charlotte le Mesure. I spent an hour and a good deal of coin on her hard bargain not to turn them over to the Moroccan slave traders.

I struggled to sit up again. The dizziness had subsided enough for me to swing my legs off the sofa and plant my stockinged feet on the polished floor. I heard a sound at the door and, confirming what I'd already deduced, Madame Charlotte herself walked in. To my surprise, she sat down next to me and patted my hand with a jewelled one of her own. She looked as elegant now as she had two years ago, her figure slender even for the fifty some years she carried. A black sheath dress clung to her and heeled shoes added to her already tall stature. She spoke in a lisping French accent, only partly affectation.

"You're awake. The sea spat you out, I hear."

"Who brought me here, to El Circa?"

My voice rasped and burned in my throat. I coughed and felt a gasping pain in my lungs. Suddenly I remembered the message delivered from Jem when he had handed me Flynn's precious ring. Jem had said to go to El Circa to rendezvous with Black Hal. Please God it wasn't him that saved me.

"Who brought me here?"

Charlotte didn't reply to my question, but pointed to a plate of food and a glass and bottle on the marble topped table in the middle of the room.

"When you're ready, sit up and take something to drink."

I badly wanted to ask if she knew anything of my ship, my men, but I didn't want to beg for news and have her feed me lies. I knew for certain this was no coincidence. I had been brought to the very place Hal intended to meet me. The room swayed again and I pushed down a wave of nausea. Suddenly the heavy scent of flowers and the covered windows made me feel as trapped as a bird in a net.

"Let me help you to an armchair," Charlotte said.

I waved her off and managed a few tottering steps myself. I was shocked at how utterly weak I felt. A memory of the beating waves that had almost drowned me flared in my mind. There was a light tap at the door. Charlotte hurried over to it immediately and without another word, let herself out. A young man walked in, followed by three others. I cried out as one of the men threw the bolt across the door and stood in front of it.

"What the devil?"

The young man, who seemed to be their leader, snickered.

"What do you want with me?" I said. "Did Hal send you? Is this a trap?"

Instinctively I reached for my cutlass but of course my hand slid over nothing more than the borrowed gown.

"A trap for you and Hal both." The young man laughed openly now. "I'd like to see Hal's face when he turns up and finds I beat him to it."

His face swung into sharp focus and I remembered. My heart plummeted in my chest.

"Cain Welles."

Cain had been one of Hal's protégées. He was a runaway from a destitute farmer's family, and was vicious and scheming even at age twelve when I'd last seen him just four years ago. Now here he stood, large as life. He wore a green jerkin and red neckerchief, his shirt unbuttoned to show a bare and scrawny chest. I noted with horror that he still wore the necklace Hal had given him on his first day aboard. It was strung with a twisted nugget of Spanish gold, fossil bones and a couple of teeth from a captain Hal had killed the day before.

"Captain Cain to you. I run my own ship now."

Cain had always been skinny but he'd toughened, taking on a more wiry look. His lean face may once have borne a wholesome farm boy's features but his innate viciousness had flourished under Hal's tutelage and turned him almost saturnine. I drove down my fear and did my best to outface him.

"How did you come by a vessel of your own? As I recall you didn't know one end of a ship from the other."

"A lot can happen in four years. After all, you turned yourself from Hal's doxy to Queen Meg of the Night Wing."

The look of spite on his face made me blanch.

"Tell me what business you have and let me out of this room."

"That's no way to talk to your rescuer. Ain't you just a little bit grateful I fished you out of the waves, Meg?"

"It was you?"

"A couple of my men did, to be truthful, but under my orders. The ruse worked a treat, didn't it? It was me that dressed the old galleon to look like Hell's Mouth, and you swallowed it, hook and line."

Cain sat down in the armchair opposite, crossed his legs and leered at me in a way I remembered only too well. On Hal's ship he had been too young for the whores so he became a Peeping Tom. You never knew when his jeering face might turn up, or where. A feeling of dread built in my chest. With these unbidden memories, others would follow. The idea of being in the power of someone who knew me from that nightmare time was more than I could bear.

"You've enjoyed your laugh," I said. "Now, what do you want with me?"

"The fun hasn't even begun." Cain crossed and uncrossed his legs. One of his men, thick set and weathered, prowled the room, touching this and that. "I been hearing about your deeds, Meg." Cain unfurled his skinny frame from the chair and walked a few steps to the table and back again. "You took down the General." His voice rasped with excitement. "Do you know that villain had me whipped? He accused me of stealing something out of his cabin, as if I would have taken a pair of candlesticks, not worth my while. I told him who'd done it and he had me whipped anyway."

I stood, wordless.

"Cat o'nine, and salt water thrown on for good measure," Cain said.

"The General was a hard man."

"He was a murdering black bastard. I would have cut his throat while he slept except Harry would have come after me. God knows what pact they had between them." His face split into a malicious grin. "But we've both left Hal far behind now, ain't we Meg? And the General even further, ocean's deep." He peered in my face. "How was it when he died?"

He knotted and unknotted his fingers. A drop of spittle formed at the corner of his mouth. I tried to hold his gaze but glanced away before I fell into the tunnel of madness behind his eyes.

"He cried and pleaded," I said, giving him what he wanted. "Wailed for his mother, like all cowards end."

"How did you do it, Meg?"

"Ran him through, clean as a whistle."

"You should have made him suffer."

There was an edge of disappointment in his voice.

"Oh, he suffered. He watched me cut down his crew and claim his precious ship."

"You could have keel-hauled him, let the sharks come."

The air in the room was tight with my dread and his madness. I had to take a grip of this if I was not to go mad myself, if I was to live.

"He wasn't worth my spending the time." I turned, adopted a sword fighting stance and parried forward. "A flick of the wrist." I danced a step sideways. "Like spearing a lizard." I parried again. "Like snuffing a candle – poof!"

Cain laughed. "A fat black lizard."

"Squashed. Crushed on the deck of his own ship in front of his men." I swung around and flung myself in the chair opposite where Cain sat. "Now tell me your plans, Cain. I confess I'm intrigued."

"Drink a glass with me, Meg."

Cain gestured for one of his boys to pour the madeira.

"Gladly. It's thirsty work telling of a good butchering."

Cain laughed again. His fingers went to the bone on his necklace then he wiped his palms down his jerkin, leaving a stain of sweat.

" How many pirate ships did you take, Meg?"

"A dozen, maybe twenty." I took the proffered glass and gulped down half the ruby liquid. My throat burned like dry kindling and the drink did little to steady my ragged nerves. Cain was mad and ready to kill me on a whim unless I figured in his plans, whatever they turned out to be.

"I heard it was more," Cain said. " I heard you gained an armada that stretched to the horizon on a full day's sail."

"There were a lot of ships, a lot of dead captains. But I traded and sold. I didn't want the ballast, it slows you down."

"Speed and freedom, that's you and the Night Wing, eh, Meg? Hal always said so. 'If I can tame that bitch, I can tame anyone,' so he told me."

Cain's smile was suddenly as innocent as a summer's morning, but it chilled me to the marrow. I stood up on pretext of pouring myself more wine. Cain stepped up behind me, touched my neck. I made myself turn to face him, smile. He regarded me then went back to his chair.

"Mostly I thought to lure you," he said. "I knew if I could gain your attention and a little time to consider, I'd win you over." He fiddled with the bone necklace again. "I've been doing a bit of commandeering myself, Meg. Not in your league of course, but I had the fortune to burn and sink two ships captained by Sanchez Banda. Wind and luck on our side. I took Sanchez prisoner and dealt him such a pretty death in front of his men that they all surrendered. It tripled our crew so I led a raid on the port at Islas Terros."

I was impressed in spite of myself. "There's a prize."

Cain nodded vigorously. "You know, don't you? The straits near Terros hold the key to a secret trade route if only someone could unlock it."

I met his gaze then quaffed the rest of my drink.

"The port's under my command now," he said. "So far, other pirates are keeping their distance but they're sniffin' around. They're not sure whether to attack or join me."

"It seems you have yourself a fine challenge."

I could smell the sweat off him, sense the fist of his madness clamped on my throat.

"So I put out a story." Suddenly, coming to the point of it, he was calm. "The word is that you and I have joined forces, as revenge on Hal and to form a pirate fleet that no one can rival. The other pirate captains can join us or be hunted down – simple. That's what they ponder on, Meg. Don't you think it's a fine tale?"

"Except pirates are not a breed that likes to serve one master. And it takes some believing that you could really hold Islas Terros."

I instantly regretted my remark. Cain's face darkened with temper.

"Don't mock me. I'm not a boy for you to sneer at."

"I'm not sneering. Merely pointing out the nature of pirates."

"I don't like this." Cain got to his feet. He turned to the older of his companions.

"Edwin, Meg doesn't believe me. How can I make her understand?"

I interrupted, desperate. "I'll believe you if you take me there."

Cain stood up, walked over to me and leaned over my chair until we were almost nose to nose. I knew if I didn't keep my nerve, I would be dead meat. I spoke defiantly. "If I'm to build this kingdom with you, I need to see it with my own eyes."

Cain squeezed my arm, too tightly, once, then let it go. He nodded. "Quite right, Meg. Seeing's believing. We'll sail on tomorrow afternoon's tide."

"Yes. I forced excitement in my voice. "I can follow you in the Night Wing."

Cain's eyes narrowed but I pressed him, as Queen Meg would do.

"My ship, if she survived, and my Quartermaster Flynn. You have him prisoner, I take it?"

Cain dealt me such a blow I was sprawled on the ground, head ringing. Edwin was on me, twisting my hands behind my back, his fetid breath on my cheek. Cain leaned over me, shouting.

"Forget all that! You don't need Night Wing or those dogs you call a crew. You are my consort now. We are to be wed, how do you like that for a scheme? You'll use your sea witch magic to find a passage through the strait and we'll be richer than any other pirate before us. They'll bend their knees, all of them, to Pirate Cain and his Queen Meg."

Cain pushed Edwin off me and dragged me to my feet. His hands held my face close to his. There was lust in him, but not for me. He didn't want Meg, he wanted power, pure and simple. I swallowed bile in my throat at the feel of him, this parasite, picking the life from everything he touched. At least it was clear. He would keep me alive as long as I served his purpose. Therein lay my hope for any chance to escape his clutches. I mustered all my courage to answer him boldly.

"You talk long and loud. If this kingdom you boast is real and true then Queen Meg will take hold of it with you and gladly." Ignoring my throbbing head and pounding heart, I held out a hand to shake the deal, a firm gesture that disarmed him. He gave a sudden grin.

"That's my Meg. I knew you'd see things straight."

CHAPTER 36

When Charlotte brought me supper a few hours later, I begged her to give me a dress, hat and shawl, together with free rein of her powder and rouge. I also pleaded with her to let me go free but she would have none of it. Her mouth pursed in sympathy but her arms were fully crossed on her bosom.

"I'm sorry for you but it's more than my life or business is worth. Cain's boys would tear down the hotel, and that would be the least of it. But I'll give you some clothes and welcome."

It was a maid who brought dresses and a box of paint for my face, and a burly man with her in case I strangled the girl and made a run for it. After they locked me in again I threw myself on the bed and cried it out. I was still weak from being half-drowned so I forced myself to eat every scrap off the supper tray before falling into a sleep.

The next morning I woke late but at noon, when Cain came to fetch me, I had transformed myself from his woebegone hostage to Queen Meg once again. A peacock blue gown and gaudy slippers were topped off with a wide brimmed hat and knotted gold and turquoise shawls and beads. To further exaggerate the fanciful ensemble I painted my face in the semblance of an Egyptian queen. Cain's jaw hung slack when he opened the door and saw me standing, arms akimbo, in the centre of the rug.

"Fast sail to our kingdom," I said.

Cain laughed, rubbing his hands in anticipation.

"That's it, Meg, that's it. King and Queen of our own dominion!"

I was escorted to portside in a covered coach. After that, Cain paraded me on the deck of the Sea Sprite to the whistles and halloos of his crew. I waved and sashayed, playing the part of his wild and exotic Queen Meg, witch of the sea, and all the while trying to catch a glimpse of the Night Wing in case she was berthed close by. But I never saw my ship. The tide turned and we set sail, my mind and heart clutching desperately to any shred of hope I could come by. I will survive this, I told myself. There will come a chance if I can hold out long enough and not become as lunatic as Cain Welles.

I noticed a few useful men among Cain's crew, but there were a fair number of dregs too, some of them obvious thieves and murderers. I was glad to be locked secure in the cabin below, though it stank like a cesspit. I was also glad the men had brought half a dozen whores on board, not for the women's sake, poor doxies as they were, but for the men to keep their thoughts off me. I had to play the Queen, Cain's intended, and hope to heaven that playing kept me alive until we reached landfall.

The next day, Cain had me brought up on deck again. Two ornate chairs were set on the bridge. There we sat to be waited on by the ship's cook, a startlingly handsome Spaniard.

"This is Nestor," Cain said. "He's sworn to my good service, ain't you, Nestor?"

Nestor bowed deeply though his look simmered with loathing. I wondered if he would make an ally.

Cain whispered in my ear. "He's mine until I give him his sister back." He winked and tapped his nose.

I nodded and smiled to cover up my rage. He was nothing more than a loathsome dog. I wondered if I could persuade the crew to mutiny. Surely even the worst of them could see there was no good or profit in his service. As Nestor served the last dish, I leaned forward to speak to him.

"You're a fine cook."

Nestor's look was so contemptuous, I thought he would spit at my feet. He covered it with a bow and disappeared below decks.

"There'll be a storm and strong winds tomorrow," Cain said. "But today is a calm sea and just the occasion to make good my promise to fair Queen Meg."

For a sickening moment I thought he was going to wed me then and there, but the situation wasn't quite so fatal. Cain got down on one knee in front of my chair. He took my hand and slid a garish ring on my betrothal finger. His expression was almost coy.

"Now we are promised. On the day we arrive in Islas Torres we'll be married."

He set off the cheering himself then bade the fiddler to play a jig. Luckily, I wasn't called upon to dance. I felt so ill with dread I wasn't sure I could even stand. The ring hung cold and heavy on my finger. Cain, seated beside me again, kept picking up my hand to admire the ruby stones.

"It will look well against your wedding ring."

I smiled weakly. I couldn't imagine anything looking well against these oversized jewels in their tasteless gold setting.

"The wedding ring is something special," he said.

"I expect nothing less."

Cain grinned. Unable to keep his secret he leaned close to whisper in my ear.

"I stole it from Hal. It's solid silver, one of his favourite prizes from a raid in Marseilles. He cut off the merchant's hand himself."

I nodded, remembering. It was the truth. Hal loved silver. He kept boxes of it, trinkets and coins. The thought of Hal and his avarice sunk me even lower. To distract myself and stop Cain from saying any more I clapped and laughed through another tune from the fiddler. A few of the crew danced. A tall buccaneer broke from the crowd of men and the few whores who watched and drank at the side of the deck The man stood in front of me, swept his hat from his head and gave a deep bow.

"Queen of the ocean!" I saw he was quite drunk. "Dance a measure with me. Our captain mustn't keep you all for himself."

Two other men from the watching crew joined him.

"Dance on our deck and bring fair weather, mistress."

A small cheer went up. I forced a smile and glanced at Cain. He had a face of thunder. The buccaneer stepped forward, clutched my hand and tried to coax me out my seat. In the next moment, Cain was behind him, a dagger at the man's throat.

"Leave her be."

He wheeled the buccaneer around to face him. The man staggered then put up his hands in a gesture of surrender. Cain pointed his dagger around the circle of silent, watching men.

"She's mine. The keys to my kingdom. Anyone touches her and he's a dead man. Say 'aye' if you understand me."

A resounding chorus of 'aye' filled the breeze. Cain swung, agile as a cat, on to the buccaneer's back and drew the dagger blade straight across his victim's throat. Blood spurted as the man tried to gurgle a sound. He fell with a crash and lay, limbs twitching, on the blood-stained deck. I stared ahead of me, impassive. I could have been back on Hal's ship. Cain stepped over the dying body and took my hand to help me to my feet.

"Apologies for my crew." He gave a formal bow. "Rough trade, some of them."

I nodded, my movements as stiff as his. Beneath my mask I felt sick to the stomach. Cain escorted me below then hesitated at my cabin door. I braced every nerve for what must surely follow, but he merely took my hand, fingered the betrothal ring for the hundredth time and bade me a good night.

CHAPTER 37

Killing the buccaneer left Cain in a black mood. He still paraded me on deck every day but was threatening and hostile to any of the crew who looked me in the eye, let alone approached me. Most of the time I was kept below in the increasing squalor of the cabin. I tormented myself with self reproach that I had been fool enough to walk into Cain's trap in the first place. Worse, I could think of no plan that would bring me to freedom.

We were barely half way through the eight week voyage when a draining apathy overtook me. I slept away most of the daylight hours while night time saw me sitting on the untidy bunk, listening to the fights and drunken carousing of the crew below. These night disturbances worsened as the voyage went on.

Cain was a terrible captain. He inspired no loyalty and his discipline swung between neglect and vicious, random punishments. I sank into despair, unable to think in a clear line. The truth was, I didn't want to think at all. I had no wish to open the floodgates of memory, to dwell on the fate of my ship and crew, though I ached to know if any had survived or if my reckless actions had murdered them all. I was tormented by anxiety over Flynn. Cain refused to speak of him, so I had no idea if he was captured or dead. I couldn't bear to rest my mind on Daniel at all. Buried deeper still was the spectre of another time of imprisonment, my sojourn under Black Hal after he had abducted me. That was a memory I could not afford to face.

The next morning, realising I was sliding to a point of no return, I dragged myself awake and paced the two strides of the cabin, up and down, desperately trying to conjure any scheme or possibility. Perhaps it was fate because when my breakfast arrived as usual, it wasn't delivered by Cain or his sour-faced bosun Edwin, but Nestor, the handsome cook I had met on deck that first day. The door was unlocked by a crewman I didn't know. He pushed it open and stood back to let Nestor walk in. The cook put the tray down on the cluttered table without a glance at me. It was the faintest glimmer of a chance. I leapt from the bed and caught Nestor at the door.

"Take this filth away!" This for the benefit of the crewman who stood a few paces away, head bent under the low, swinging hammocks.

Nestor's face stiffened. He stepped back inside the cabin to pick up the tray. I brushed close to him and whispered. "Where is he holding your sister?" Nestor stared at me, doubtful, eyes flickering with fear. I pressed him. "Do you think I want to be on this stinking ship, prisoner to a madman? We can help each other. Is there a chance of raising mutiny?"

I had his interest now. He shook his head then craned his neck to see if the other crewman had heard us. I thrust the tray into his hands and spoke loudly. "Bring me something I can eat and get rid of this pigs' swill?" He fumbled with the dish and glass. "Can you write?" I said under my breath. He nodded briefly. "Then send me a note with the next meal."

Nestor backed out, his eyes never leaving mine until he had closed the door. The key jangled in the lock. My heart was jumping like a hunted fox. I had taken a frightening risk. My mind filled with visions of Nestor running up on deck to report my treachery to Cain. I kept reminding myself that Cain needed me for his grand plan, for now at least.

I passed the next hour in dread then with more calm as the clock ticked away an hour more. The night passed as usual, though I received no message with the supper tray. Cain was much as always the next day, surly with his crew but courteous enough to me. I heard nothing from Nestor for the next two days but on the night following there was a small roll of parchment inside the napkin on the tray of food Edwin brought me. I tucked the parchment in my gown. Edwin didn't linger but, to be sure, I waited until the empty tray was fetched away and the night watch began before fingering the roll open to examine it by the light of three fresh candles.

The note from Nestor was written in black ink and a small, even script. 'He says my sister is in Malaga, in a house where he stayed, near the Basilica. But I fear she is already dead at his hand. Her name is Silvia Cardenas. If you find her, save her. I will smuggle a copy key to your cabin. Before we dock in Torres the ship will anchor in the Bay of Palmas for one night while the Captain sends in his spies. That is your chance to jump ship. Find Silvia or the devil haunt you.' He signed it 'N de C.'

I burned the parchment over a candle flame then lay on the bunk, my mind whirling. If I could be free of this cabin, if I could sneak on deck, slip overboard without being seen. If and if – but a chance of sorts, the only one I had. It was a small and desperate plan but it kept me alert and alive through the next tedious weeks of the Sea Sprite's voyage. I made my plans as though I would succeed in my escape. I would need money for bribes, a dagger and clothes that would disguise me as a boy.

I stole a handful of coin and jewels from Cain's treasure box the one night he invited me to sup in his stinking cabin. The room was lined with every sort of musket, rifle and cutlass. He had always loved weapons of any kind, the more exotic the better. I managed to ask Nestor for the boy's clothes and dagger and, one week from Islas Torres, he arrived at my cabin door past midnight, wild with fear, to press a bundle of cloth and the duplicate key into my hands before locking my door again and running off. I stared at the key in my palm. I had no idea how he had managed it, through bribe or threat or if he'd stolen it from Cain's own key ring.

My luck held. On the evening we sailed into the bay of Palmas, Cain brought me up on deck to gloat about how close we were to our goal.

"See that line of trees and the tall rocks beyond?" He pointed to the land mass at starboard. "The fort is a mile from there. It's a fine setting for our marriage vows and where a hundred pirates will gather to bend the knee to me and my Queen!"

He gripped my arm with excitement.

"At last," I said.

He nodded. "At last. The bay's deep so we can come close in. My men will scout for villains and dissenters so we can be sure of safe landing. I want to arrive in pomp and style at the fortress steps."

I nodded but my eyes were all for the string of rocks that formed a necklace from ship to land. I was confident I could swim the distance to shore in the calm, warm water of the bay but it was reassuring to see there were resting points should I need them. A rowboat full of spies was put out then I was escorted back to my cabin. I sat for a full hour until the candle guttered and the noises of the ship settled. I readied the boy's garb I would soon change into and checked my bundle of dry clothes, dagger and jewels. Wrapping them securely in sealskin, I tied them with a piece of cloth torn from my bed sheet.

The sight of land had heartened me and, though every nerve stretched with each passing minute, I felt a blaze of excitement at the prospect of carrying out my daring plan. For a week I had moved the key from one hiding place to another. Now I checked it once again, nestled in the box of tallow candles. There was a thud against my cabin door and the jangle of keys in the lock. I almost jumped out of my skin before I realized it would be my late supper tray.

The door flew open, Nestor lurched towards me and fell with a crash to the floor. I stifled a scream, both hands to my mouth. Nestor's face was bloody. One of his own cooking knives stuck out from his throat. Behind him was Cain, Edwin and a bully of a sailor called Jericho. Cain's face was white with rage. He stepped over Nestor's body and grabbed me by the hair. I fought him off, taking him by surprise. Edwin came after me, hauling me to the floor.

"Bring her!" Cain order was a strangled shout.

Someone threw a blanket over my head. The two men half dragged, half carried me through the main deck to Cain's cabin. The door slammed shut and the blanket was pulled away. I stood facing Cain. He sat in his chair behind the narrow table that ran almost the length of the cabin. Like everything else in the squalid room, the table was littered with clothes, bottles, coins and half burned candles. There wasn't a book, map or ship's chart in sight. Cain had never been a natural sailor. It would be so easy for a navigator to trick him off course or into an ambush, I wondered it hadn't happened before now. His reputation for viciousness had kept him afloat but it didn't make him less stupid when it came to seafaring matters. I let the wave of contempt buoy me up, a little way above my terror.

Cain never took his eyes off me. "Edwin, search her cabin. If you find anything amiss, large or small, bring it."

Edwin left and Jericho shifted his position to stand guard behind me, holding my arm in a bruising grip.

"Have you something to tell me, Meg?" His voice was so pleasant he might have been remarking on the weather, but I saw the rage nip his cheeks white. I kept my mouth shut.

"Why, Meg?" He leaned across the table towards me. His eyes were like stones. "Didn't I promise you a kingdom? The finest promise you've ever had and you spit it back in my face." His fists slammed the table then his hands spread, fingers working back and forth like tentacles against the grained wood. "You stand there, high and mighty, but I found you out. The cook, that black dog, copied the key to your room so he could board you every night. I was polite, good to you, I respected the future Queen of the Islas, and all the while…"

He sat back, speechless with rage. The door opened and Edwin walked in. I could sense his hot excitement without looking at him. He placed my carefully packed bundle on the table. Cain snatched it and unrolled the oilskin to uncover the stolen dagger and jewels. The air was tense, ready to burst like a bubble of foam then Edwin leaned forward again and carefully placed the duplicate key beside Cain's fingers.

"I found it hidden in the candle box."

I felt Jericho take in a sharp breath. As for Cain, he stared at the key for a long, stretched out, moment.

"Betrayal, Meg." His voice was laden with disappointment. "Here's me thinking you was just making sport with the ship's handsome cook and all the while you're scheming to run and leave me."

He got to his feet. His fingers slipped around the hilt of his cutlass, agitated, around and around. I could see the effort it took him not to strike me down where I stood. I struggled against Jericho's grip, every instinct seeking the dagger that lay on the table, one stride away. Jericho tightened his fingers. I winced in pain.

"You will marry me." Cain's voice was like ice. "Tomorrow, you'll be my queen, for all the pirate world to see. The captains and buccaneers are gathering even now. They'll sign their oath at the wedding feast and you'll be there to strike fear and faith into their black hearts." He looked me close in the face, his body still, his expression quite mad. "With their pledges I'll rule the oceans. After that, I won't need Queen Meg. You'll get the end you deserve."

He shoved past me and flung open the cabin door. "Well done, boys. How about you have her, as a reward?"

Edwin looked astonished. Jericho's hands gripped, loosened, gripped again.

"But she's to be your bride," Edwin said.

I felt myself about to faint.

"Do you think I care to touch her now?" Cain danced a stride towards me, like a striking snake. Clawing the neck of my gown he tore it open a few inches. "She'll always be Black Hal's whore." He spat on my cheek. "Don't mark her though. No bruises or broken bones for the wedding day, if you please."

With that he was gone.

I wanted to become a dead woman, a creature of no feeling. But I was there, in Cain's cabin, I, Queen Meg and Margaret Robertson both, trapped in her prisoner's body while Cain's men had their way with me over that terrible night. It is one thing to observe a man's character from a distance, but quite another to experience their worst traits first hand when given the licence of secrecy. They urged each other on, taunted and railed at me, or however much of 'me' was there to react to their vicious acts.

At one point Cain returned and I was galvanised with fresh horror that he might take part. The sight of him perched on the table, sipping a cup of wine, his eyes glittering with lust and revenge, broke open the worst memories of Hal. I believed I had hidden those recollections in a chest of iron and dropped it to the pit of the bottomless ocean but that night I remembered it all.

In the end, Cain left without a word and the others soon after. I lay on Cain's bunk, staring at the patch of dark night through the cabin window. Little by little the dark faded to pearly grey then opalescent blue. Dragging my stiff limbs from the bunk, I pushed open the tiny window to inhale the sweet smell of warm ocean. Whatever fresh horrors lay ahead, the night had brought me an unexpected blessing. Cain's men had dragged me to a nightmare I had lived once before. Within that nightmare I discovered fourteen year old Margaret Robertson had not died at Hal's hand after all. She had lived. Now she and I could go on together.

CHAPTER 38

Once a grand gateway, the fort at Islas Terras was now broken and dilapidated. I gazed at the crumbling stone buttresses as we glided past in the row boats. One of the pair of huge oak doors hung askew, sewers ran direct into the sea from the rear walls. As for the sailors who manned the entrance and courtyard, they were the dregs that you saw washed up at every port in the world.

I was decked in a glittering gold and black dress, my face painted and a heavy veil covering my head and shoulders. Edwin had brought the dress to Cain's cabin that morning, along with a bowl of mutton stew. I hadn't looked at him but afterwards I had washed myself and eaten the stew, astonished at my own calmness. Now, here I was, approaching Islas Terras and marriage to Cain.

As we approached the fortess steps, a brass bell rang out in the watchtower. There was a crowd from the doorway to the wharf, mostly sailors and their women and a few townspeople. Cain had gone ahead in the first boat and was waiting for me at the top of the steps. Beside him stood a frightened priest. All I could think of was Daniel, how I had forced our would-be marriage on that drunken night. Daniel had been my prisoner, just as I was Cain's. At least I had set Daniel free but he had suffered nonetheless.

Cain ran down the steps to meet me. He took my hand in a tight-fingered grasp. I saw his look of satisfaction as he gazed over my extravagant appearance. Leading me up the steps we faced the priest together and Cain lifted the heavy veil from my face. My exotic makeup and braided hair made him smile in spite of himself. There were astonished and admiring gasps and glances from the crowd. When he looked back at me I saw it in his eyes. His rage at my betrayal was wiped away. I was his Queen Meg, fulfilling his dreams, his stepping stone to the throne of the seven seas.

Cain took off his tri-cornered hat. He wore a purple silk waistcoat that went ill with his complexion. In spite of his finery, he still wore Hal's bone necklace. He nodded at the priest and I realised with a shock that he was to marry us right then and there on the steps. The ceremony began. I was stifled in my heavy dress but beneath it, I felt cold as stone with a heart to match. The bells pealed again and I watched Cain's mouth as he intoned the words the priest gave him. I followed suit. What else could I do? In my mind it was Queen Meg who was being married. Margaret Robertson was safe, held in the tiny flame that had blossomed in my chest since daybreak.

Cain placed the heavy silver ring on my finger and held my hand aloft to the cheering crowd. Another roar went up as barrels of ale and wine were rolled into view. Arms linked, we led the press of people through the fortress door to where a wedding feast was set up in the courtyard. Musicians struck up a reel and Cain led me in a few slow-paced country steps before bowing to the crowd and guiding me to the head of the two long tables.

The noon bell chimed and the wedding feast was in full swing. The first guests were pirate captains. More arrived as the afternoon went on. There was dancing and a drunken brawl. Food was thrown from one end of the tables to the other. All the while I sat like a painted doll, unable to muster a coherent thought. I knew it was aftershock from the night's horror. I was glad of the numbness. I doubt I could have survived the day otherwise. More visitors arrived, another long table was brought out, more food heaped on platters.

As the sun began to dip and deepen to red, Cain called Jericho over. He whispered something in his ear then banged on the table to get everyone's attention.

"Honoured pirate guests!" He got clumsily to his feet. "You've done yourselves a favour coming here today. Pledge to throw in your lot with me and Queen Meg and enjoy the protection and the spoils of our new kingdom of Islas Terros!"

He pulled me to my feet then walked me the full length of the courtyard. Torches were being lit all around us. Jericho was ahead. He carried a tall backed chair with a velvet cushion on it and set it down in full view of the tables. Cain seated me there and left Jericho standing guard over me. My body trembled at his proximity as I remembered the outrages of the night. Cain walked back to his seat, stopping to take a piss behind his chair, like the ill-mannered dog he was. He spread his arms with a flourish and shouted.

"Queen Meg!"

Someone called out. "Have you found the hidden trade route, mistress?"

Cain interrupted. "Of course she has. As soon as my darling Meg was within twenty miles of the bay, she knew it, smelt it on the westerly wind. We'll be rich beyond counting."

A stocky captain seated close to Cain stood up to make his voice heard. His frock coat was a few sizes too large and a gaudy red. "The western current's a death trap. How will it carry us to the path of the merchant ships and not run us aground?"

"Faith, Captain Stark," Cain said. "Faith in the witch of the seas." He raised his arm and pointed to me. "Queen Meg's judgement never goes amiss. Has she ever been shipwrecked, sailed a wrong current, missed a fair wind?"

As if to illustrate Cain's point, a gusty breeze bent the torch flames and whipped the pennant flags strung at the fortress gate. There were murmurs and a ripple of uneasy laughter. By luck, Cain had picked his moment. Evening clouds raced in the sky and a flare of sunset lit the fortress battlements. I watched Edwin hand Cain a rolled parchment. Cain unfurled it and held it up to flap in the wind. He called out over the wind.

"Your oaths, gentlemen! Every Captain shall sign his pledge here, tonight, to join our fleet and share in the treasure haul."

He passed the parchment to his left. The first few pirates signed with the quill and ink Edwin gave them but the next, a rough-looking brute dressed in a pilfered dragoon's jacket, waved a refusal. Cain frowned at him.

"Jack Merritt, don't you want a share of the new kingdom?" The words were polite though there was a nip of rage in his voice. Merritt spat in his hand and stretched across the table to offer it to Cain.

"That's a good pirate oath," Merritt said. "Blast your fancy parchment and pen." He looked around the tables. "Half these dogs can barely write their names anyway."

A few men protested. I saw one loose his sword in his belt. Cain climbed on the table and knelt on it in front of Merritt, grabbing the man's collar. "If you don't like the ink, you'll sign in blood." His dagger was in his hand, glinting against Merritt's cheek. Merritt leapt back and threw the man next to him across the table towards Cain. A fight broke out and Cain was on his feet, kicking at the head of one of Merritt's defenders.

I sat like a stone, watching Cain's dream begin to fall to pieces as soon as it had begun. I sensed the wind lift and swing around from the west, bringing with it the scent of sweet ocean. It was as though I woke from a dream. Blinking my eyes, I looked again at Cain. Everything was sharp as a pinprick, Cain's angry, frightened face, the brawl of men around the table, the dogs guzzling the food that had spilled on the pavers.

Cain screamed something. Suddenly, the shadows of running figures were all over the courtyard. Jericho took a step forward, his sword at the ready. He was half a pace in front of me and there was no one at my other side. I slid off the chair, gripped it by the back and lifted it. Either the chair was lighter than I 'd estimated or I had recovered my strength. In any case, I picked it up easily. With a wide swing I smashed it into the back of Jericho's legs. He went down, cursing. The moment of freedom went to my head like strong wine. I picked up my heavy skirts and ran full pelt to the shelter of the inner wall. My freedom was short-lived. Hands caught and held me fast and I was fighting for my life. I kicked and twisted, rage and panic gasping in my throat. A voice hissed in my ear.

"Hold, mistress. It's me. It's Flynn."

CHAPTER 39

I gasped and craned my head to see my captor's face. It was Flynn indeed, as if risen from a dream.

"Quickly!" He pulled me towards the open fortress doors.

Needing no encouragement, I ran hard beside him. I was in a daze of shock, disbelief swinging to relief and back again. At the door, two other men joined us.

"The alarm's about to go up," one said. "The boat's waiting."

Flynn pulled off his long jacket and helped me drape it over my head and shoulders. The jacket smelled of sweat and the sea, and of Flynn. I clasped it tight as he and the other men formed a group around me and pushed through the milling crowd to the fortress gate. From there, they half carried, half dragged me down the steps to a waiting boat. I was hoisted aboard, the boat rocking violently as they jumped in after. I heard musket shots and shouts of alarm. One of the boatmen cried out.

"Hell's breaking loose!"

I heard the creak of oars as they dipped and turned us sharply into the bay. Dragging the jacket from my head I saw a blaze of fires around the fort and dark figures running everywhere. There was more gunshot, whether at us or not, I couldn't be sure. In any case we were quickly out of range and Flynn's men were rowing for our lives.

"I have good news for you, ma'am."

"Seeing you is the best news I could wish for."

"Ah, but this may top it. I saw it with my own eyes. Cain run through with a dagger and shot with a musket for good measure. You're a widow."

A bubble of hysteria rose in my throat. Cain was dead and I was free. I slumped back against the boat rail, speechless.

"There's more, ma'am. I have a ship." Flynn paused. "I have the Night Wing,"

I placed my hands in a silent prayer on my heart, and to hold the wild bird that was beating its wings in my chest.

She was right as rain. My ship. Still, it was a bitter-sweet reunion as I boarded her, knowing most of the crew had perished in Cain's deadly ambush.

"Almost every man drowned," Catter said.

"But not you." I took his proffered hand to climb from the top of the rope ladder and on to the main deck. I embraced him, something I had never done. Awkward, he patted me on the back.

"Not me, nor Jed Burnett, nor Pedlar either."

Tears started as I came face to face with Pedlar himself. His familiar shock of red hair and broad grin had never looked so much like a miracle.

"You're a sight for sore eyes."

Pedlar bowed. "As are you, ma'am. We've made your cabin clean and ready. Flynn swore he'd get you back and we believed him."

Just then Flynn himself appeared beside me.

"We'll cast anchor and away," he said.

"Without a word to tell me how you fared in England, or how you came to my rescue?"

It was only then I realized what was different about him. He had grown a full beard since he'd set off for England to take Daniel to safety.

"As for the last, it was easy," he said. "Cain put out such a broadcast that every pirate for a thousand miles knew of his marriage to Queen Meg."

I wiped my face and bit my lip to stop my mouth from trembling. My nightmare was over. My limbs fell slack with relief. I looked up at a scatter of stars in the night sky and the thread of clouds scudding across the waning moon.

"It's a fair wind west." I looked at Flynn. "Shall we sail through the strait?" I laughed at his surprised expression.

"Are you telling me Cain's boast is true? The sea witch has found a safe passage to the fair ports west?"

"I can see it and I can smell it. We'll stitch a fair line through the straits and beat the currents if we're quick about it."

"Then we may as well pick off a merchant vessel on the other side," Catter said. "They'll never see us coming."

I nodded. "Yes. It's a fitting voyage for Queen Meg's return to her Night Wing."

Flynn turned to one of the sailors. "Fetch Jack Lance," Flynn ordered.

"Jack Lance is here?"

"Poring over charts, ready to impress you with a perfect route east and to safety. Remember, he and Joshua went inland to explore the country, and thereby escaped a drowning."

"It fills my heart to know they're both saved. Tell Jack to bring the charts to my cabin. We'll plot a route west together."

Flynn and Catter took up positions on the bridge. The light from a swinging lantern caught the gleam of eyes and the gestures of hands, pale against the dark. I stopped myself from interrupting them to ask about Daniel. That young man's life was none of my business now. Flynn would have told me if anything was amiss. I pictured Daniel, safe at his father's table, and wondered for the thousandth time if he thought of me and the Night Wing.

Casting fantasies aside, I stooped my head and set foot on the ladder to go below deck. Before I took another step, the list of the wind changed a fraction. It was like the moment when the first warmed cupful from the pump gives way to a cooling draft. I shivered with excitement, sensing the current of the sea join with the fresh night air. I ran back to Flynn and called out.

"Sail, Quartermaster, full speed into the strait, while the wind is behind us. It's now or never."

Flynn didn't hesitate. He left the wheel to Catter and jumped off the bridge to stride along the deck, barking orders. I relished the sounds of the crew calling back and forth as they hoisted and pulled, the creak of ropes and the flap of sail. The Night Wing leapt in to full flight.

CHAPTER 40

It was a close call but we threaded a straight way through the straits. The wind urged us all the way, before it suddenly turned and dropped. As we emerged into open sea we sighted a merchant vessel, fat with spoils. I pinched myself for luck. The ship would be oblivious that any pirate could slip across its path so many miles before the known geography of land and current made it possible to do so. We took her clean and quick. I should have gloried in our easy catch but as we fired our first broadside I felt myself sick and almost faint. I motioned to Flynn.

"Do the honours, Quartermaster, if you please. The past days' events seem to have caught up with me."

Flynn stepped up to the bridge to give the orders following the attack. I hurried below decks to take refuge in my cabin. They had spread bunches of dried lavender around the room and it was every bit as spick as Catter had promised. I sank into my chair, sliding my hands along its familiar warm wood. Gunshots and shouting echoed overhead, and the rip of the sails as they billowed in the changing wind.

I felt sick to the core, and frightened. This was far from my usual glee at taking a merchant ship and its cargo. I had completely lost the stomach for it. It was then I realized Queen Meg had been dealt a blow when she'd seen her own pirate reflection mirrored in Cain's evil face.

Margaret Robertson, sheltered in a fine home home until that terrible day, had been fashioned into Black Hal's creature. I saw it most clearly, the life of a pirate was no noble venture, it was murder and thievery. Queen Meg had escaped from Hal's grasp only to live the very life he had forced on her. I had careered across the seven seas, taking everything in my path, driven by an appetite for plunder and conquest whose true purpose had been to stop the yawning blackness inside me.

I leapt to my feet and ran to the basin, retching bile and the remnants of my wedding feast. The fit passed as suddenly as it had come. I drank a cup of water and climbed on my bunk to open the window and listen as the merchant captain parlayed long and noisily for his life. Flynn would spare him and throw him off the next port with a few provisions. Meanwhile, he would pressgang the merchant's crew for the Night Wing, load our fresh plunder on board and sail ahead until we found the next ship to prey upon. It was thievery, even if Queen Meg had never been as merciless as Hal and his like.

I lay on my bunk, watching the sun's bright climb in a cloudless sky. We had taken the merchant at dawn and now it was late morning. I roused myself to change my clothes. The glittering pile of fabric that had been my wedding gown lay on the cabin floor like the peeled skin of an exotic snake. I washed and dressed in men's clothes except for leaving my hair in braids and painting my face afresh with gaudy green around the eyes and vermilion lips. As weary as I felt, I had to keep Queen Meg alive for the crew.

I went above deck where Flynn and Jack were eating bread and cheese at the capstan near the bridge. They were arguing over the return route. I interrupted them.

"We can't go through the strait from this direction."

"Try telling him that." Jack pointed his jaw at Flynn.

"We can't just sail on the main route," Flynn said. He gestured to the merchant ship, still in sail, following on our portside."We'll be picked up by other pirates waiting in ambush for ships like this one."

"Where do you propose we head for?" I said.

Jack interrupted. "That's for you to say, ma'am."

I looked at the horizon, shining blue in the early afternoon. There was only one place on earth my mind could fix on. I turned to Flynn, unable to stop myself.

"How was England when you left?"

"If you mean Daniel Stede, he was delivered safe."

I saw him and Jack exchange a glance. A moment stretched out. It was Jack who broke the silence. "Shall we look at the charts again?"

"The devil with your charts," I said. "What news of Daniel that you're not telling me? Is he ill? Or married?"

"His father did mention a cousin within minutes of his son walking through the door." Flynn gave me a strained look. "But I believe they've been too preoccupied to make wedding plans."

"Have you taken to speaking in riddles? Tell me now, Flynn, and tell me straight."

"He's afraid you'll turn us full sail to Cornwall," Jack said.

Flynn scowled at him, then placed a hand on my shoulder as if to steady me. "Black Hal is raiding the coast from Tintagel to Port Isaac. The dog is destroying the villages, one by one, and boasts he's set in for the whole winter if needs be." He spat on the deck at his feet. "He's calling himself the King of Cornwall. It's a jest but a vile one."

"And Daniel? Lord Stede? Has Hal attacked them too?"

"When we left Europe in search of you, the rumour was he planned to eat up the coast either side of the Stede lands and save them till last. He needs the river access to attempt that, impossible if the towns inland are still free and able to rise to Stede's defence."

"This is about me and Daniel, isn't it?"

Flynn nodded. "He thinks he's found your weakness, Meg." I was startled by the fear in Flynn's voice and that he called me 'Meg', one of the few times since we'd escaped Hal's ship together. "Hal's counting on luring you there, with Daniel as bait." Flynn's voice turned pleading. "Don't go. You just escaped from one trap, I'm begging you not to walk into another.

Jack put up his fists as though in a fight. "If you want to fly after Black Harry, I'm right behind you."

Flynn gaped at him. "Don't make things worse, Jack."

"Someone has to stop him. What he's doing is nothing short of carnage."

I interrupted them. "You know it's me Hal wants."

"I should have killed him when we escaped his ship four years ago," Flynn said.

"Yes, but I ordered you to let him live. I had some twisted notion he would suffer more to see me gone and out of his grasp than if you'd slit his throat. You may look askance, Jack, but it's true. I've regretted it every day since, for the scores of lives Black Hal took since then. If I look in my heart, I believe I was simply too afraid to kill him. It's time I finished the job."

I gripped Flynn's hand where it still rested on my shoulder.

"Come to my cabin, we'll talk strategy, and Jack, set a course for England, as swift as you please. We'll take a risk on the trade route if need be."

Jack nodded grimly and turned back to the bridge. Flynn's head was down but he followed me below decks as requested. Once inside the cabin I sat down and gestured for him to do the same.

"I need you on my side, Flynn."

"Is this all about Daniel?"

"Not all, but I won't lie and say I don't want to protect him. And the innocent people that deserve a life free of Hal's evil. But this is mostly about a girl named Margaret Robertson."

Flynn looked startled, as well he might. I hadn't mentioned my real name to him since we'd run from Hal's clutches.

"He took that girl when she was barely fourteen, slaughtered her family and broke her life. He bonded her to him, like an evil father. It haunts me that this was the real reason I couldn't watch him die. It seems like madness to speak of out loud but Hal was all I had for those years. He taught me sword craft and the ways of the sea. He was devil and father rolled into one."

Flynn looked at me as if for the first time. I heard the breath in his chest and throat. He reached across the table for cups and jug and poured rum for us both. Slowly, he raised his cup in a toast.

"To the end of Black Hal," he said.

I tapped my cup against his and drank the full measure down.

CHAPTER 41

I wanted to sail direct to Cornwall's north coast to hunt down Hal, fast and hard, but my better sense prevailed. To win this war I would have to take the path of strategy and caution. Apart from a brief skirmish as we joined the trade route, we had the good fortune to sail a free voyage south. I felt strangely calm. It was as if the horror of being kidnapped by Cain, assaulted by his men and coming so close to a grisly death by his hand, had rinsed me clean of anything but a deep determination to face Hal once and for all.

On that voyage, thoughts of my parents came unbidden. I suffered nights of crying for their loss. It was a grief I had been too frozen to feel. In one evil hour, Hal had destroyed them and I had been powerless to avenge them or protect myself. Now, I was powerless no longer. I kept Cain's wedding band, the silver ring he'd stolen from Hal, on the window ledge in my cabin where it was in plain and constant view. It served to remind me that I was Hal's trophy no more.

On a cold dawn in September we anchored a mile offshore, close to Par harbour. Catter took a boat and went with instructions to beg, borrow or steal a horse. After that he was to ride hard and convey a message to Lord Stede. Assuming Stede accepted my offer of assistance, he would rendezvous with us at a hidden cove that Flynn knew from his smuggling days. It seemed an irony to be parlaying with Stede once more, but for such a different intention. I hoped the Lord's famous stubbornness would bend enough to at least hear Catter out and, with good grace, accept my plan.

I fretted on board for two days. Flynn judged it time enough to set off for the rendezvous point. We travelled under cover of darkness, Flynn, Jack Lance and I. Dropping a row boat in the slow waves off the point, we plied eastward along the coast. We fetched up in the tiny smuggler's cove where our meeting with Stede would take place. The cool dampness of the air had me shivering under my greatcoat. Seagulls keened as the first grey light of dawn broke through the wreathing mist. Flynn saw them first.

"They're here before us."

It was the first words any of us had spoken since we'd made shore.

"Looks like two men," Jack said.

I felt stupidly nervous at the prospect of facing Stede. I could only imagine what he thought of me, his son's kidnapper. The two figures came into sharp focus as they left the mist behind them, but the man walking behind Catter wasn't Lord Stede, it was Daniel. I felt a shock go through me. Of course I had hoped to see him again, but it hadn't occurred to me that would be today.

Daniel strode towards me and held out his hand. He looked older and somehow stronger, as though he had come into his power as a man in the weeks since I had seen him. His face was more strikingly handsome than I remembered. I was torn between shyness and a desire to throw myself in his arms.

But I too was changed since our last encounter and it was with a sober nod that I returned his handshake.

"Mr Stede."

"Mistress Meg."

The tone of his voice, warm, cultured, brought a familiar rush of feeling. He spoke confidently.

"My father's been unwell and still not recovered. It's been an uphill battle but he's entrusting more of the day to day running of the estate to me."

Flynn stepped past me to throw an arm around Daniel's shoulders. "Ruling the roost, eh?" They both laughed. I was shocked at how familiar they were with each other. It occurred to me they must have bonded as friends on the voyage back to England. I was beset by a confusion of feelings, and jealous of their easy camaraderie.

"You'll want a few minutes alone, I dare say," Flynn said. He cocked his head at Catter and Jack. The three of them walked some paces off, away from the shore line. I was flustered, unprepared.

"What the devil is Flynn playing at?"

"He's right," Daniel said. "We need to talk for a moment."

"We need to talk about Black Hal, and the present danger you and your estates are in."

The breeze whipped my damp hair across my cheek. I pushed it back.

Daniel cleared his throat. "I have something to give you." He reached inside his coat and handed me a small, square object.

I took it automatically and found myself unwrapping a book from a piece of linen cloth. The book was slight, with a green binding. I opened the cover. There was her name, written in a pretty flourishing script, written by her to mark ownership of her book of drawings and pressed flowers, on a day long ago. Margaret Robinson. I felt my heart break open, the shield I would need to face Black Harry shift and waver.

"No!" My gasping shout made Flynn and the others turn their heads to look. "This isn't the time Daniel. I don't know where you got this from but it isn't the time." I was close to tears.

"Then when?"

"After I've dealt with Hal."

"Are you sure?"

"You think he will get the better of me? Finish me off?"

Daniel tried to take my hand. My own was shaking. I moved back a pace.

"I made investigations, discovered where you and your family used to live," Daniel said. "You haunted my thoughts, Meg. I had to know about you. Your house was gone of course, razed to the ground in the fires that Hal spread through the village and estate. Anything worth salvaging had been carried off long ago, but I went to visit the parish church, to ask about the raid, and the priest had this." Daniel tapped the book gently. "He came across it in the churchyard a couple of days after the pirates had gone."

The memory was sweet, like a dream. A white dress, a bunch of wild flowers, my quill broken and cast into the grass as I waited for my parents to finish talking to the other parishioners after the church service. I must have left the book too but there was no time to remember it or anything else, because the raiders came not long after we returned home. And now the girl in the white dress was standing in man's garb with her crew of pirates, planning to face the man who had taken her life away from her.

I looked up at Daniel. His face was etched shadows in the dawn light. I would have done anything to throw my arms around him and hold fast, never to let go. But the spectre of the past, of Black Hal, of the woman he had made me, stood between us. I could not avoid the reckoning that I had to face, not if I was to have any sort of peace, with or without Daniel. reached out and took Daniel's hand, like a starving man snatching for food. I kissed his palm then pulled back and took a few steps towards the ocean. Long shallow waves dragged the pebbles whispering back and forth.

Catter called out. "Are you all right, ma'am?"

I waved to reassure him. Wrapping the book in its linen cloth, I tucked it inside my coat. I still couldn't take it in that Daniel had cared enough and thought enough about me to search out my past and bring me such a precious keepsake. After a few deep breaths to stop my tears, I walked up the beach to join Flynn, Catter and Jack. The scrape of Daniel's footsteps on the rough stones followed me.

"Tell us your news of the raids, Daniel," Flynn said.

"Hal's men burned the cottages at Levington on the coast west from here. They stole everything they could carry then disappeared again. It's a pattern he's repeated over, a raid and destruction to follow, then," he clicked his fingers, "they vanish."

"We need to discover where he's bolting to," Jack said.

"Every time the militia come or we send search parties, we draw a blank. Hal simply disappears into thin air."

"That's where I come in," I said. "Queen Meg and the Night Wing are bait that Hal won't resist for long." I turned to face Daniel at last. On that cold beach with the threat of Hal nipping at our heels I saw the love in Daniel's eyes. It seemed impossible it should be this way, yet there it was.

"Can you buy us a ship?"

"Another ship, Meg?" Daniel's face broke into a grin. "If I can get the money from my father, which, this time, I think I can."

"Convince him the Night Wing will lure Hal into an ambush where your ship can help us finish him off."

Daniel paused. "He remembers your father. When I told him of your family, he said he had served on the assizes with him in Truro. He thought him a decent man and condemned Hal for his treatment of you."

The idea that Lord Stede knew my father caused a further breach in the wall I had built against remembering the past. "Next, you'll tell me he's forgiven Queen Meg for kidnapping his son," I said, to make light of it. "Jack, go with Daniel, help him find a ship and crew. We'll anchor the Night Wing on the north coast where we planned. It's imperative you get to us in three or four days. I don't want to play sitting duck any longer than that."

"You're really putting yourself out as bait for Hal?" Daniel said.

I nodded. "He can't fail to hear of the Night Wing, especially if we make a show of it as we sail along the north coast."

"You're risking an awful lot."

"As long as Hal doesn't attack the Night Wing before Daniel and Jack arrive with the other ship." Flynn sounded as concerned as I've ever heard him.

"He won't. He'll be keen to taunt me first, make a chase of it. That should buy us time."

I shook Jack's hand and led Catter and Flynn back to the rowboat without looking at Daniel again. I couldn't bear a formal farewell. For all my bravado, I knew this game with Hal was a deadly one.

CHAPTER 42

It was a nerve racking business, sailing the treacherous currents around Land's End on our circuitous route to the north coast. Every moment I searched the horizon for the black sails of Hell's Mouth, fearing Hal would come at us on the open sea before we were ready for him. The weather was cold and, though I slept little, I spent the three nights' voyage in my cabin, bundled in blankets with heated stone bottles pressed to my back and feet. By the end of the week we passed Trenance and anchored just off the point. We kept the pennants flying to make sure the passing vessels could mark us as the Night Wing. According to plan, we truly were sitting ducks. Hal couldn't fail to take the bait.

The morning we anchored was on a day full of sea fret that bobbed and jerked the ship. I went up on deck to watch the silver flecked waves slap against our timbers, the clouds fluttering like grey ribbons in the wind. Catter joined me in scanning the horizon.

"Flynn isn't keen on this business, ma'am."

"I know. He fears Hal's aim is to capture me again. But he shares my regret that we didn't finish Hal when we had the chance. It would have saved scores of lives."

"I relish the pirate's life," Catter said. "The adventuring, the riches to be gained. But I hope someone runs me through before I become a pitiless dog like Black Hal."

A cry came from one of the ship boys who was leaning over the prow. "Boat!"

Catter and I ran to the starboard where the boy was pointing. A small boat of four oars came alongside and soon we were helping Jack and three of his new crew aboard. Jack was grinning from ear to ear.

"Lord Stede coughed up the money as Daniel promised. We have a fine sloop, the Fancy, fully crewed, fully armed and anchored just around the point in the next bay."

I clapped him on the shoulder. "You weren't seen?"

"We were quiet as could be, ma'am. It's hard to conceal such a venture but I don't think there's many who would turn spy for Hal these days. Even the worst port villains have had enough of his antics."

"Is Daniel on board?"

"He went back to his father after we purchased crew and ship." I felt a stab of disappointment. Worse, a fear that I might not see Daniel again. I squashed the feeling and brought myself back to the matter in hand. "Take a bite with us before you go back to your new command, Captain Jack."

"Begging your pardon, I'd like to stay here on board the Night Wing, if it's all the same to you. The Fancy is in safe hands. We have a very able captain in Grant Recarson. I knew his brother, he shipped for the Marlin when she was afloat. Recarson knows what to do when Hal attacks. It's a simple manoeuvre for the Fancy to nip around the bay and close in, but more difficult for the Night Wing if Hal meets us head on. I'd like to be on hand to help."

"As you will, but come and take a sup in any case. We're all starved in this cold weather."

We went below to eat hot stew and fresh greens and talk over the ambush plans again. We laid it out on the table, with plates and forks used to stand in for the vessels and their sailing routes. As Jack said, it would be simple for the Fancy to hold Hell's Mouth in a pincer grip if we were quick enough to manoeuvre the Night Wing on their starboard side.

We spent the rest of the daylight hours on deck looking for any sight or sound of Hal. We waited for three days. My nerves were rubbed raw with speculating on every bad outcome. On the evening of the last day, Flynn went ashore and came back with news that Black Hal had destroyed a fishing hamlet some twelve miles west. Three families had been massacred, their boats towed out to sea and burned. It took all my will power and Flynn and Jack's reasoned arguments to stop me going after the villain then and there.

"It's what he wants you to do," Flynn said. "You knew this is how it would go."

"Damn him to hell and back. What if he keeps this up all winter long?"

Flynn shrugged "Even Hal must tire of goading you sooner or later."

I had an unbidden memory of Hal in the first weeks of my capture. He had brought me a kitten and said he would give it me as a present, though I wanted no such thing. I wanted to go home, even though my home was burnt and gone. He threw the creature overboard in front of me. I bit my tongue bloody so as not to give him the satisfaction of my tears. I cried less and less after that day and at last not at all.

"I hope you're right, Flynn."

"He haunts my dreams too, ma'am, but he's only a man when all's said and done. We'll get him, I promise."

I put a hand on his arm in acknowledgement. Flynn, above anyone, understood about Hal and the grip he had had on me. He had been press ganged to crew on Hal's ship and seen me and other young girls brought on board as prisoners and sport for Hal and his men. In a way I was lucky Hal had taken such a liking to me, at least it protected me from the fate of many of the other girls. Some had thrown themselves overboard or lost their reason.

I went below deck to distract myself by reading my books and puzzling out the sea charts Jack had sketched. There was something amiss that I couldn't place my finger on. And it still wasn't clear where Hal had his bolt hole. Nothing made sense whichever way you looked at it, charts or no.

Two days a later, a fishing boat washed up in the bay that lay to our west. The bodies of two fishermen lay in the boat's bottom, their throats cut. I went ashore to see to their burial myself. There I heard the men were casualties from an attack by Hell's Mouth on a village some eight or nine miles away, close to the border of the Stede's estate.

This time I had no blazing urge to run after Harry. My resolve was hard as flint.

"He'll come soon and we're going to have him," I said to Jack. "I feel it. He can dodge and weave all he likes but the Night Wing draws him close. He won't be able to help himself."

That night I stayed on deck with the watch, wrapped in blankets and with a cup of madeira to warm me. Since Daniel had handed me my keepsake book and spoken to me of the past, I had fought to keep a lid on the memories that threatened to overwhelm me. Now, standing at the port side of my ship, my senses keen for sight or sound of Hal, I let loose my grip on those haunted thoughts and allowed the past, the memories of my childhood, to surface and encircle me.

At first it seemed more than I could bear then, as the tears came, I retrieved them, one by one, the golden days that had belonged to the girl I had once been. I ran with my dog, Tiger, to the stream below the paddock, throwing sticks in the pebble strewn water. My mother stood in the kitchen on baking day, instructing the cook as she floured her own hands. Another memory rose like a bubble to the surface of my mind. Our steward's son, George, taking me out in his fishing boat. He would steer the tiny vessel, gravely, expertly, and drop a line to lure pollock and King. Afterwards, with a pail of fresh catch, he would sail around the coves, dodging neatly between the rocks and currents.

"Do you feel that Miss Margaret? How the breeze changes shape a second before the pull of the ocean switches us out to sea and in again?"

I would close my eyes and nod and smile because I truly could feel it, every breath and tug just as he described and more. I wonder what George would have thought to see me now, my hands gripping the freezing rope of my own ship's mains'l. The rope was slack, waiting for the hoist, but my past had nudged into the future. The smell of the night breeze and the prickling on my neck told me Hal was coming.

CHAPTER 43

"Jack!" I called.

He left the bridge and ran the deck to reach my side. I pointed nor'west.

"He's coming fast, this way."

I felt calm, drained empty by my grieving for the past.

"Hell's teeth! Can we turn the ship and set sail in time?"

"Set to it Jack. I'll raise Flynn."

The stillness of the night shattered as the crew raced into action. By the time I was back on deck, a bleary-eyed Flynn pulling on his coat behind me, the breeze had taken the sail and our ship was turning in the water. Jack had despatched a rowboat to the Fancy to warn her to stay hidden and at the ready.

We were quick but, in the last hour of night, under the moon-filled sky, the Hell's Mouth came bearing down on us like a swooping eagle, black sails flapping. The first cannon shot came before we were fully on course. The race began as we tried to push the Night Wing hard across the path of Hal's ship before he could inflict a direct hit. We almost made the turn when I heard Catter yell.

"The Fancy! She's come too soon!"

Dawn was breaking. It was all too easy to make out the Fancy's prow and sail as she edged around the coast. Of course, Hal saw her too. His crew must have thrown themselves to oars and sails because they were turning hard about at speed, ready to make a run for it before we could trap them between our two ships.

I laid hands on the ropes myself as we flipped course and made a beeline for Hell's Mouth. Between Jack's steering and Flynn's goading the crew, the Night Wing leapt to a speed that seemed impossible even to me. We closed on Hell's Mouth inch by inch until we were close enough to hear their ropes creaking. Hal's crewmen shouted and cursed as they struggled to keep ahead of us while readying their weapons for attack. A blazing firepike soared in the sky and plunged into the sea, missing the Night Wing by inches.

Suddenly, I spotted Hal on deck. He was bare headed and wore a soldier's crimson jacket that stood out like a flag. I focused on it like a beacon, willing the Night Wing to gain on him, force him up against the Fancy and make an end of him. We were closing fast. Hell's Mouth fired a volley of molten shot and iron that hailed on our decks in a deadly storm, bruising and burning half a dozen of our men.

Catter yelled from the foredeck. "Do we turn about, ma'am?"

"Never!" I had fixed on that crimson jacket and the black heart that beat beneath it. Nothing would turn me aside now. I ran to the bridge, in full sight of the labouring crew. "The dog shall have his day in hell!"

The order went below decks for the oarsmen, if they could find it in them, to quicken their pace even more. Now we were in a straight line for the starboard side of the Hell's Mouth while the Fancy was closing in on their port bow. Another rain of shot scattered on the deck, blowing a hole off the Night Wing's bow rail. The crew had their wits about them this time and no one was harmed. I stayed on the bridge and took the spy glass from Catter's hand. Putting the glass to my eye and turning the cylinders, I brought the red-coated figure of Hal into sharp focus. I could see the grim set of his features, his mouth barking orders. He ran the ship's wheel himself. It looked as though he was trying to bring his ship hard to starboard and out of our reach, but it was too late. We had him.

I took off my hat and raised it high in a triumphant gesture. The movement caught his eye, standing as I was in full view, against the backdrop of the clear morning sky. Hal gave me a lewd and vicious gesture then disappeared from the deck. If he had gone below to urge his own oarsmen, it was a wasted effort. In moments, our grappling hooks hit the timbers of the Hell's Mouth, the ropes were secured and the first of my crew were swarming across the gap. I readied myself to follow them but Jack intercepted me.

"Not yet, ma'am. There'll be a bloody fight when they land on deck. Don't risk your victory with your life."

He was right of course. I schooled my patience and stepped back. I still held the icy calm that had overtaken me when I felt the breeze that was the messenger of Hal's approach. Uppermost in my mind were the faces of the two murdered fishermen as we laid them to rest. I swore it would be the last crime Hal would ever commit.

As my men boarded Hal's ship, the Fancy, now in range, began to rain shot and musket fire from the port side, offering a distraction that allowed my men to make a swift victory. From the melee of fighting on the Hell's Mouth deck, a white flag of surrender was thrown up the mast. The battle was over.

I felt curiously distant, unable to grasp that this was one of the most important days of my life, the day when I had turned the tables on Black Hal. I turned to Flynn who had waited beside me while the boarding took place.

"Bring him," I said.

Flynn took off, his tall frame climbing, agile as a monkey, across the taut ropes until he could leap on the deck of the Hell's Mouth. I went to check on our own wounded, who were lying in a bath of blood and cannon shot at the far end of the deck. One was a young pirate who had been enlisted by Flynn at Cartagena. He was in a bad way, his right leg blasted off, his face white and feverish. I kneeled in the blood and took his hand.

"Jeremiah Dunn," I said, remembering his name. "Hold fast."

He nodded, his mouth quivering, sweat beading his cheeks. "Is he served, ma'am?" Have we done for Black Harry?"

"He will be, never fear. His ship is captured. The Hell's Mouth won't sail under him again. The Quartermaster has gone to take him prisoner and bring him aboard."

Jeremiah nodded then grimaced with pain.

"I hope I live to see it, ma'am."

"Your leg is gone," I said. I pressed his hand more tightly. "But there is a tourniquet to hold the blood and you suffered no other harm. All will be well."

"My mother. She'll look for me."

I kissed his forehead. His eyes closed, whether to open again, I could not say. I stood up to watch as four of the crew took Jeremiah and the other wounded below. One of them returned to swab the deck just as Flynn clambered back across the ropes. I ran to meet him.

"He's gone," Flynn said. "Hal and his first mate, a man called Rame, took a boat and jumped ship. Two others tried to go with them. Hal ran them through and Rame pitched them into the sea."

My cold calmness deepened then cracked. My limbs shook. I remembered Rame, a tall brute of a Scot who had joined Hal just before my escape. Flynn went on, his voice grim.

"We took his Quartermaster. He was in full bile over the betrayal. He told us all without prompting."

I closed my eyes, trying to picture Hal, the boat, the drop into the ocean, the oars pushing them away from the Hell's Mouth while the fight raged on the deck above.

"Are you all right, ma'am?"

I nodded, my eyes still closed. I felt the deck of the Night Wing tip and roll under my feet, a fractional movement of the waves. My mind ran forward and I followed after.

"Find a row boat, Flynn, You and I are going after him. Bring another man, a good shot, but all discreet, and right away."

Flynn gave a frown but didn't hesitate. I ran below to my cabin to add another dagger to my belt along with the short knife and cutlass I already carried. My heart was pounding with red rage. All trace of numb composure left me. I had bent myself to face Hal at long last, to deal him the blow I should have struck four years before and the dog had thwarted me yet again. I caught sight of my reflection in the glass. I was shocked to realise I wore no makeup, that the face looking back at me was young. Not as young as Margaret Robertson nor so worldly wise as Queen Meg, but something in between the two.

"He has both of us to contend with now," I said.

I raced above deck to find the boat was let down already with Flynn at one oar and a crewman I didn't know the name of at the other. The vessel was the smallest we had, useful for scouting close around the bays. I hoped it would be up to the task I required of it.

"I'm Ralph, ma'am," the crewman said. I dropped into the boat alongside them. "Flynn picked me as being the best with a musket."

I nodded to him. Flynn cast off. A couple of the crew watched us from over the side but no one called out.

"I put it out that we were going aboard the Fancy," Flynn said. He added, lightly. "Where are we going, by the way, ma'am?"

"Following Hal on the cross current." Flynn stared at me, hearing the excitement in my voice. "Take oars, gentlemen, turn about and row to the north side of the prow of the Hell's Mouth. When we are a quarter mile beyond, ship oars and wait."

"A quarter mile on open sea, in this?" Flynn sounded dubious.

When I made no reply, he shrugged and set to turning the boat. I took an oar myself, more to feel the flow of the ocean through my fingers than to force us along. What I had sensed up there on the deck of the Night Wing had no reason to it, but my instincts shouted at me to follow. Now, down in the water, on the lapping waves that rolled higher as we pulled further away from the Hell's Mouth into the wide ocean, I had a moment's black doubt. We breached the strong current running east, dangerously shipping water as our small craft rolled on the wave's edge.

I held my nerve. We quickly lost sight of land or ship then suddenly I felt it, like a darting fish in the water beneath us, a fine cross-ripple in the ocean's tide.

"Hold oars!"

Ralph and Flynn looked at each other, as well they might. A sailor's instinct would be to bend deep into the strong current, use its force to carry us towards the west. Instead, we lurched and bobbed on the waves before spinning a half circle again towards the southeast. Flynn looked as nervous as I'd ever seen him. Waves were building to the north of us. At this rate we'd be picked up and rolled like pebbles on a mountain side.

Our narrow prow, light as a rag on the deep sea, locked into the rogue cross current and we suddenly leapt forward and darted on a course back to shore.

"Row!" The boat skimmed the waves like a bird as it danced us back to Cornwall's coast. "Hal's been sailing north then heading back on this current with a small boat as guide and docking again right under our noses." My voice strained above the blustering wind.

Flynn gave a curse. "He was lucky to catch on it today."

Ralph nodded agreement. They were both breathless with exertion in the aftermath of fear and effort. But Queen Meg heard the ocean and knew she had Black Hal in her sights at last.

CHAPTER 44

We fair sped to the shore, a small cove where waves broke on a ring of jagged rocks. We had travelled east at a fast pace and the curve of land behind the beach and the hillside beyond suddenly looked familiar. I realised with shock that we were barely ten miles from my childhood home. It seemed as though everything conspired to draw me back there, Daniel, Hal, even the pull of the sea. My chest shuddered as I felt the land fold me in a deep embrace. Whether I lived or died today, I was where I belonged. Hal had failed to take everything from me after all. My soul and heart remained.

We shipped oars and let the current guide us neatly between the rocks. The ocean was deep up to the shoreline in the cove. It was a perfect hiding place in which to moor the Hell's Mouth. Perhaps Hal had discovered it years ago and hidden here before he raided my village and home. The tiny beach dipped a sharp slant into the water that allowed the boat to run itself aground. We jumped out and dragged the boat up the sand in case the tide turned. Flynn already had his cutlass drawn though there was no sign of boat or men. I pointed to a low line of broken cliffs ahead of us. Clouds blew in, the sun disappeared and the air took on a fresh chill.

A shot rang out. Instinctively I dropped flat to the ground. Ralph crouched next to me, fumbling in his pouch for powder to prime his musket. Flynn was out of my line of vision, I guessed behind the upturned boat. I heard the faint scratch of a pebble behind me and swung around to find myself looking up at Hal's first mate, Rame. The devil knew where he had sprung from but his eyes were already bright with triumph.

Rame's musket was pointed straight at my skull. I kicked forward with both feet and Rame's next shot exploded in Ralph's chest. Ralph's uncocked musket fell to the sand and the weight of his body after it. I scrambled to draw my cutlass before Rame could leap for me. Suddenly, Flynn appeared behind him and spun a glancing blow at Rame's back. The blade cut but the stout leather of Rame's jerkin stopped a fatal blow. With a shout of agony he dragged his rapier free and hacked about him. Flynn had come too close. He took a terrible cut between his shoulder and neck. Blood spurted as he lunged forward. Before I could leap to standing and deal Rame a blow myself, Flynn had dealt him a deep blow to his unguarded chest. Rame fell to his knees with a groan then gurgled his last breath as his head fell forward to the sand.

"Flynn!" I caught him as he swooned forward. Throwing all my weight under his unharmed shoulder, I dragged him to standing. "Run! With all your strength."

He pumped fresh blood with every step but I had to get us under cover. Where Rame was, Hal would be close. We stumbled into the first cave beneath the cliff. As Flynn slid to the ground I untucked my skirt from my belt and tore strips from the hem to make wadding and a bandage.

"We have to wash it, did you bring rum?"

Flynn tried to point to his jacket, but he was too weak to manage even the
that small gesture. I pulled his flask from the pocket and set to work. My fingers moved automatically, binding, tying, my mind lifted above the bloodstained cave floor and Flynn's body like a dead weight. I had never seen him wounded beyond a scratch, not in all the battles we had fought together.

"Go, Meg." His voice was a bare whisper. "Finish him. Take the muskets."

"They're no good, Flynn. Damp from the soaking we had in the boat. Ralph didn't stand a chance." I felt tears rise. Flynn's chest laboured under my hands as I tied the last of the knots on the makeshift bandage. "He should have taken more care, and now he's paid for it. The harsh words were my way of steadying myself. If I thought of Ralph's honest, brave face, eyes still open and turned to the sky, I would have been undone.

"He's up there somewhere," Flynn said. "That black bastard. Did I tell you he took a woman and drowned her, just because he knew I liked her? My kisses were her death sentence, Meg."

"He took a lot of women," I said, fearful that the beginning of delirium was taking him. I grasped Flynn's hand. "Look at me, Flynn. He won't take this woman. Not today."

I splashed a measure of rum over the wound before he could think on it, then put the flask in his good hand. He tried to raise it as though in a toast.

"To you, Meg. God protect you."

I touched his face and got to my feet. I wouldn't let myself fall with grief or fear. I would hold my terror and my rage and use them to sharpen my senses. I didn't look back at Flynn as I left the cave. I could do nothing more for him except save us both from Hal.

Edging along the rocks that strewed the bottom of the cliff, I craned my head, searching for any sight of Hal. Suddenly, from above, I heard the scrape of a pebble on rock. I knew with every fibre he was there.

I stood still, looking up, thinking my way back to him, to Hal, my abductor, the black and tainted man who had called himself my lover and father both. I had learned to read him when I was his captive and now was the time to remember again. I imagined him in my mind's eye, crouched on top of the cliff, watching, listening. He would wait for me and Flynn to go back to the boat then he would rush us, cutlass and dagger flying. He never trusted firearms but always surrounded himself by men who could wield a musket. His firearm was the firepike, the brute force of a molten hot grappling hook thrown on the deck of his captured prey.

He may not know how badly Flynn was wounded. Even now he may be wondering if Flynn was climbing the cliff to attack him from the rear. I drew my cutlass and weighed it in my hand. It slipped with sweat in spite of the cold day. He wouldn't expect me to go directly after him, so that was what I must do.

I slipped off my boots and proceeded in my stockinged feet to pick a silent way up the slope. Halfway up was an overhang where I crouched to get my breath. My eye caught a flicker of something dark, a shadow or glimpse of foot or sleeve, directly above. I waited. A seagull keened, swooped the cliff and flew out to sea again. I suddenly thought of my home, not the Night Wing but the house of stone and wood I had grown up in. I remembered the orchard and paddock and fields stretching to the shore, to cliffs such as this one.

I edged a few steps until I was under the very lip of the overhang. The grass-covered ledge stuck out beyond, like a finger pointing out to sea. Hal wouldn't fail to see me there. I walked on to the narrow platform, turned around and looked up. I startled him. He darted backwards, disappeared for a moment then his head and shoulders emerged again. He had discarded the crimson jacket. His sweat stained shirt was an old calico such as I'd often seen him wear. Emboldened that I'd fired no musket, Hal came to the edge of the cliff and looked down on me.

"I have your ship," I said. "And your first mate is dead."

I pointed to the body of Rame on the beach, my eyes never leaving Hal's face. I had to remind myself that he wasn't as tall as he first appeared, nor as strong. He was a cunning rat who surrounded himself with stronger, more able men to do his work.

Hal wasn't, nor had ever been, handsome. His dark, mean features were pocked and blistered by years of weathering on the open seas. But he had a force of personality like the devil himself. I used to think it was my youth and fear that had put me so deep under his sway, until I saw how he managed it with everyone who came in his vicinity. Once he gained even a finger of power over you, the depth of menace in him held you like a fly in a spider's trap. I fought it now, the pull to be persuaded by his piercing expression or by the incongruous gaiety of his gestures that could almost have you believing you and he were having the best time in the world rather than facing off as mortal enemies.

"Meg," he said. "Has it come to this?" He laughed suddenly. "I knew you would come back to Cornwall to rescue your pretty young man. Why, Meg? Did you think you could become a dry-land wife? What sort of love did you hope to have with him? I know you for the cold bitch you are."

I bit my lip, refusing to be goaded.

"I heard you married Cain, and killed him too."

I remained silent, watching.

"Do you want share of the plunder, is that it?"

He crouched on his haunches and smiled down at me as though relaxing for a tavern gossip.

"We've had a fine game of cat and mouse these last years, haven't we Meg?" He slapped a hand on his thigh. "I've spawned plenty of bastards in my time but you're the nearest creature living that's like my own child."

The quiet air billowed around us, pulling in and out on the ocean's quiet breath.

"You took me from my home," I said. I was startled at my own clear voice. "You destroyed my family."

"You've destroyed plenty yourself, Queen Meg. We're all killers at heart."

He unfolded his legs to sit on the ledge that overhung the grass platform. I knew he was positioning himself to strike yet I was unable to make a move. I was paralysed by him, mesmerised as I had been all those years I'd lived on his foul ship. Terror mounted in my chest. My years of buccaneering fell away and I was fourteen again, snatched, half grown, to be this man's creature.

His eyes never left my face as he slid from the ledge to land two yards in front of me. I took a step back, my instinct halting me before I went off the edge.

"Come, Meg! The Night Wing and Hell's Mouth together, what a fine sight that would be. I'm proud of you, four years off on your own and you make yourself Queen of the seas. I shout a toast every time I hear of your conquests." His face took on a sly look. "Especially when you killed the General. He'd grown too big for his boots, but you took him down a peg, down to the ocean's bottom." He laughed, a hollow sound. Rain spattered my face as the breeze lifted, sending clouds racing. His outright lie broke the spell. He would never celebrate the General's death. The villains shared a strange, deep loyalty born of a history no one knew about or fathomed.

"Flynn!" I shouted, hoping to distract Hal for a second.

"Your man's wounded, I think," said Hal. He never took his eyes off my face.

He stepped lightly towards me. In the next second his rapier lashed out, knocking the cutlass from my grasp. I let out a wail of anguish and bent forward, my arms wrapped around my body as though to hold in my grief and pain.

"There, Meg."

I could hear the surprise in Hal's voice. Since the first weeks of my capture, he had never seen me cry. His hand touched my shoulder. I smelt the smoke of the ship's battle still on him and the sourness of unwashed clothes. I leaned into him a fraction, as though yielding to his comfort. My hand grasped the dagger, hidden at my waist. Firm, I stabbed him in the arm then low in the ribs. Hal dropped the sword. He roared with pain as his uninjured hand fastened a grip on me like a vice. His breath laboured as he pulled me into a terrible embrace and tried to pin my arms.

I lost control. Screaming every foul name I could lay my tongue to, I drove the knife deeper in his ribs. He coughed, stumbled, almost taking both of us over the cliff. Bracing my knee against his thigh, I plucked myself and the dagger away. His hand still grasped at my arm as the other clutched at his stomach.

"You're a damned whore! Meg."

His voice slurred as his weight fell against me. His hand was at my breast, clawing to my throat. I wanted to push him off the cliff or walk away as he died in agony on the grass, but I couldn't. For me and for young Margaret Robertson I had to be sure that Hal was dead, that he would never rise again to take another of his nine lives and haunt me once more.

"No!" I said. It was the only word I could find. "No."

I dragged myself from his grip, stepped behind him, pulled back his head and drew the blade of my dagger across his throat. His steel grey eyes opened wide to the sky as they had done a thousand times on board the Hell's Mouth. He didn't need to look for wind or tide to carry him on this voyage. I let go the weight of his body. It fell to the grass, blood blossoming from his wounds. I wiped the knife and stuck it in my belt. Gathering a handful of stones I scattered them across Hal's chest.

"For my father and mother," I said. My voice was a croaking whisper. "For all the souls you hunted and harmed. May we find peace."

CHAPTER 45

I stood for a while as the racing clouds passed shadows over Hal's body, watching death turn his face to grey. At last I turned away and, with limbs that weighed like lead, I climbed slowly back down the slope. I didn't think I had it in me to look at Flynn, but of course I must. I pulled on my boots and made my way back to the cave.

Flynn lay where I'd left him, still as the stone floor. I leaned over and touched his face. His skin was icy cold. I had a strange urge to make him comfortable, though he was beyond comfort now. Pulling my scarf from around my neck and my jacket from my shoulders, I tucked the garments around him as though to keep him warm. I wanted to speak to him, tell him that Hal was dead, but no words would come. With Flynn and Hal gone, the nightmare years of my capture had been blasted apart and I stood alone in the wreckage.

I knew if I stayed and gave way to the tide of memories, the adventures and madness that Flynn and I had shared, I would never rise again. I touched Flynn's cheek, his hand, then stood up and walked out of the cave. He would want me to live, to beat Hal at the last. I stumbled to the boat then realised there was no way on earth I had the strength to haul it down the beach, let alone row it along the coast by myself. With a shudder, I saw the bodies of Ralph and Rame, sprawled on the bloodied sand. Turning to look at the sloping waves rolling in off the sea, I thought of Catter and Jack, waiting for us on the Night Wing. They seemed to belong to a dream or another life.

I turned inland. The climb uphill to the sloping fields above the cliffs took what felt like eternity. At last I was on the ridge. Clouds built and broke, and the rain came in cold showers, blown in from the sea. I set my feet on the track leading east, to Belleven, the place of my birth.

The land looked the same though every building was a ruin. I had only thought of my own house destroyed by Hal's arson and looting but now I saw how he had wreaked devastation on all the farms for miles around. He had even used gunpowder to blast some of the sturdier buildings. These were the homes of low and middling gentry, a class Hal hated and envied in equal measure.

The track followed a shallow vale. With a jump of my heart I knew I was close to the house. There was the wall, scattered boulders, a tangle of overgrown bushes and the Cornish hedge that marked the perimeter of our small holding. I stopped and took my bearings from the steeple of the parish church a mile or so to the south. The terrible events of that day rose in me. I saw my father, crimson blossoming on his white shirt as Black Hal cut him down. Smoke billowed from the upper windows as cook and the house boy ran from the kitchen door to be bludgeoned by Hal's men. My body shook as it had trembled then, my dress muddy where I fell and was dragged up the slope to be taken to Hal's ship.

It was like fighting a strong tide to stagger down that hill after so many years. My clothes were soaked with rain, my feet slipped on sodden grass. I clambered over the broken house steps and took shelter against what remained of the interior wall, somewhere close to where our living room hearth would have been. I kneeled down on the broken floor then curled against the shattered wall like an animal gone to ground. I was utterly spent, shivering with cold, grief weighing on me like a stone.

And that is where they found me, hours later. The rain had ceased and dusk pulled the few rays of a setting sun from the sky. I heard a footfall and Jack's voice.

"She's here!"

I managed to open my eyes and saw, not Jack, but Daniel. I felt his arms around me, the murmur of words in my ear. I could hardly breathe, he held me so tightly. There was no question of my walking so he carried me, back up the slope then down the steep track to the cove beneath the house. Jack talked breathlessly all the while. He told me that the militia had gone to Stede's house and were looking for pirate Queen Meg who was rumoured to have sailed the coast to join Black Hal on his raids.

"Daniel came to warn us right away. He came with me and Catter in the last rowboat and search every rock and cove along the coast. We found them, the bodies." Jack paused.

I shrank deeper in Daniel's arms. I heard him speak, as if from a long distance.

"Shush, not now. Meg, Catter is waiting with the boat. We'll get you back to the Night Wing and sail out of English waters right away."

I clutched at his jacket.

"Yes, I sail with you," Daniel said. "I won't leave you again."

Then Catter was gripping my arm and helping Daniel lift me into the boat. The rain came down again and twilight dimmed the ocean to grey. I remember vomiting over the side, me who had never been seasick in all my time as a pirate. In the shelter of my cabin Daniel helped me off with my soaking clothes and wrapped me in blankets to urge warmth into my shaking limbs. The fever was on me. There were terrible dreams, always circling back to Hal lying, eyes open to the sky, on the inlet's ridge. But beyond the horror, I felt the comfort of Daniel and of the rocking lilt of the Night Wing, carrying us to safety.

Then there was a morning with sunshine let in between the curtains and the fever drawn out of me like the turning tide. I was so weak I could barely turn my head on the pillow. In the next moment I thought the delirium had consumed me again. Where I thought to find Daniel in the chair next to my bed, my eyes rested on Flynn. I stared at him and stared and then began to cry. He pulled the chair close and took my hand. He had shaved his beard. A thick bandage covered his neck and shoulder. One arm was held in a sling and he was more thin and pale than I had ever seen him.

"It was touch and go, Meg." His voiced rasped, almost a whisper. "They didn't tell you they found me alive in case I didn't make it. But here I am." He leaned forward, gripping my hand more tightly, and planted a kiss on my forehead. "And so is my Queen Meg,."

"No, Flynn. I believe she died along with Hal. She kept me alive long enough but I can't be her any more."

Flynn squeezed my hand. "I think pirate Flynn has had his day too. Staring death so close in the face, it made me realise I've had the devil's luck all these years."

"What will you do?"

"Well, at present I intend to sail with you to Cartagena."

"Oh, that's where we're bound?"

"It is. Me and Daniel hatched the plan between us. You'll be safe from treason trials and can live with Cal's family for a while. And there's Gower too. We hear he's settled with a wife and two stepsons, and grown stout and content into the bargain."

My eyes filled with tears. "Oh Flynn, it was worse than all the rest, to see you laid cold in that godforsaken cave."

"It was the cold that saved me. It's what made you wrap me warm in your own scarf and, when I came to, what drove me on hands and knees outside to make a fire from the tinder in Rame's musket. It was the fire that Daniel spotted while they searched the coast."

"And a wretch covered in blood and looking like a ghost crouched next to it," Daniel said. He walked in, sat on the edge of the bed and took my other hand.

"Cartagena?" I said.

Daniel smiled. "I recall you thought it a fine destination not so long ago."

I groaned. "To trap a kidnapped man into marrying. Are you going to shame me with that memory?"

"Never, Meg." He touched Daniel my cheek. "I intend you to make good your threat."

EPILOGUE

We were married in Cartagena, not by a rogue of a sea captain but by a real priest in a chapel. Flynn stayed long enough to be best man before he found a passage south and to Ireland.

"There's a woman there," he said. "I know, don't roll your eyes, there have been a lot of women, but this one had a son to me. I mean to be a father to him, if she'll allow it."

So I gave him a fine pension and Cain's betrothal ring to sell or keep as he pleased, and wished him safe voyage. As for the rest of my treasure haul, I kept a modest sum for myself and the Night Wing and bestowed all else in a trust fund. Daniel and a Columbian lawyer helped me draw it up. I hoped it would help rebuild a half dozen Cornish villages and estates. I remained an anonymous benefactor but the trusteeship was handled by Lord Stede of all people. More astonishing, he'd taken Catter on as his steward and the pair were making a great success of running the estate. They also did me another service by putting it out that the pirate Queen Meg had killed Hal then been drowned by his first mate.

From such an ill-starred beginning, it astonishes me every day how deep I hold Daniel in my heart. The marriage wasn't easy at first. There were months when I thought the spectre of my ordeal with Hal would stand between me and Daniel for ever. But it was his kind gentility, the quality I had seen in him from the start, that won through at last. He was patient, he let me keep him at arm's length until I could trust again. Then the flood gates opened and I poured it all out, my terror, disgust, horror, at all that had been done to me and all I had done in return. Queen Meg was laid to rest at last.

A pirate's death had another advantage. It gave me fair chance to return to England as Daniel's bride, Margaret Stede. We both missed Cornwall and Daniel was keen to take his part on the estate and village affairs again. So, after three years, we are readying the Night Wing to sail home. I have made a few journeys in the Caribbean and fostered a reputation as a reliable and discreet merchant specialising in rare cargo. The Night Wing has been refitted of course and her name changed. I called her after our daughter, Pearl.

Pearl is two years old and I wonder if she will join me on a voyage or two when she's grown. I watch her fascination with the waves and, when the breeze changes, see her head lift and hold still as though she is listening for the shift of wind and tide.

END